THE CHIT'LIN COAST

A Tale of Growing Up Black and Female in Mid-Twentieth Century Chicago

"White folks got the Gold and Platinum Coasts in Chicago. Black folks got the Chit'lin Coast-—broke down and messed up"
-Anonymous Black Chicago Resident

L. A. Whitaker

This is a work of fiction. Names, characters, places, and incidents are products of the author's imagination or are used fictitiously and are not to be construed as real. Any resemblance to actual events, locales, organizations, or persons, living or dead, is entirely coincidental.

Copyright © 2014 L. A. Whitaker
All rights reserved.

ISBN: 150230791X
ISBN 13: 9781502307910
Library of Congress Control Number: 2014916122
CreateSpace Independent Publishing Platform
North Charleston, South Carolina

ACKNOWLEDGEMENTS

To Lauren, Wendy, Martha and above all, Al—many thanks.

PROLOGUE: 1954

When I was five, my family traveled from Chicago to The Farm, my paternal grandparent's summer home in Bridgman, Michigan. That trip made me realize, for the first time, my parents couldn't stand each other, hadn't for a long time and there was nothing I could do about it. The most important thing that trip taught me was that my family, as a concept and as reality, was unknowable and mysterious, expanding, contracting, sometimes dark, cold and dangerous, sometimes open, warm and supporting but unfailingly undependable. I saw myself for the first time, too, as an individual, an outsider, seeing, thinking, evaluating, judging life and others. Finally, I think it was the beginning of my default life philosophy—keep moving on, over, forward, no matter what happens.

I think it was the day before Labor Day, in 1954, when Dad woke us early in the morning, and crammed our pajamas, my robe and his baseball bats into a big paper bag and threw it into the car's trunk. He loaded us quickly in the car and jumped in the front seat where my mother sat frowning with her arms crossed. My baby brother, Mike, and I were in the back seat. He was only one so he couldn't kneel, but I did so I could look out the window.

We drove southeast through the city until the houses, which got smaller and smaller, started to disappear. "There's the last liquor store in Chicago! We're at Indianapolis Avenue!" Dad called out. The store didn't look like much--several filthy windows covered in pictures of bottles and cans. My mother closed her eyes.

Daddy said, "Kim, look out the back window and tell Daddy if you see any police cars. No matter how slow I drive, these peckerwood cops will stop you just because you're colored."

I knew we were in Gary, Indiana when I saw its flaming and thundering smokestacks and smelled the oily fart stink that seeped through the car doors. I hollered "P-U!" and held my nose. I lifted Mother's hand to see the time. I had recently learned to tell time so I'd know when my favorite TV show-—Pinky Lee-was on, but Mother's watch said it was only eleven in the morning, although the sky was so dark with rolling clouds of black and red smoke it looked like midnight.

Smokestacks gave way to farms with faded red barns, grazing cows and horses, and houses bracketed by green trees. The air smelled of cow manure and I gagged as the sour odor blew in my window. When I saw a thick bunch of trees coming up on the side of the road, I tapped Mother on the back. Mother spoke for the first time, "Ricky, pull over so Flower can pee."

I'm going to explain the confusion about my name right here. When I was born, my mother wanted to name me "Flower". She was an avid gardener and artist and crazy about nature. She liked delicate names that reminded her of birds, meadows, forests, water. She came from a family of popular but plain names—Anne, Jane, three Edgars-- and wanted a different and beautiful name for her firstborn, a daughter. Her name, Rachel, was always considered to be the oddest of the lot, and people teased her about it. That ridicule made her dislike her own name and determined not to pass it on.

My father, Richard, balked. He thought the name Flower was weird and neither of them was willing or able to compromise on another "nature" name. I don't know if Mother even thought of or considered any other acceptable and pleasing nature names as alternatives to Flower. Daddy suggested some of the old-fashioned female names treasured in his family—Ruby, Merle, Carrie-- but Mother strenuously objected to them. She hated what she called "old-timey" names and was in a perpetual war with his family anyway. Arguments over the name ensued and since Rachel and Richard were conventional in many ways, the vanilla winner of the name debate was "Kimberly". Nevertheless, until the day Mother died, she called me Flower and until the day my father died he called me Kim.

On the trip to Michigan that day, I ran behind the trees and Mother stood in front of me so no one could see me from the road. On these trips, we peed in the roadside woods and stopped at filling stations only for gas because my parents were afraid the gas station whites wouldn't let us use their restrooms.

When we crossed over into Michigan from Indiana, I saw our turnoff—a crooked dirt road that branched off next to a big sign that said "Knaap's Farm and Nursery." The sign showed a little blonde girl in a Dutch hat cradling some tulips. I always watched for it even though you could barely see the girl because she was bleached from years of rain and snow. But my father forgot it was the turnoff for The Farm and Mother yelled at him: "Why don't you read a map, Ricky! If you came up here so much when you were a kid, how could you forget where to turn off?"

Before I was five, I was hazily aware that Mother didn't have much to say on these trips and that she didn't like The Farm. Her complaints always centered on the dirtiness of the place and the trifling ways of Dad's family members. Sure enough, when it came into sight, she started fussing, "I hate this place. Your mother lets those boys of Tad's pee on those mattresses and doesn't change the sheets." My father never responded to her attacks on his family's housekeeping, he would just holler back as he did that morning, "You just don't like my family."

The Farm was a semi-collapsed and ramshackle two-story house that stood alone under some trees. Its exterior was brown-stained and cracked white stucco. The wood frame showed through so many of the cracks, the house's facade looked like a jigsaw puzzle with pieces missing. Its sunken concrete steps were framed by weedy patches of long-lost gardens.

It always mystified me why they called it a farm. When I was four, I'd asked my father how they could call a place a farm that had no animals--no chickens or cows, barn cats or dogs, like the ones in my picture books. Dad had smiled wistfully, "We used to when we went there every summer. It was so much fun. We played baseball all day."

That day, Daddy pulled up on the grass in the front yard of The Farm beside our uncles' cars. I started to jump out. "Leave the pajamas in the car. They'll just get bedbugs in them if you take them inside that house," Mother warned. I could see my older cousins playing piggy—-backyard softball--on the sand lot at the side of the house. My father grabbed two of his bats out of our trunk and headed off to talk briefly to my grandfather and his brothers, who were sitting in their usual spots around The Well. Then he ran over and tossed the two bats to one of the girls, my older cousin Peanut, chunky and boyish.

Mother sat in the car and I saw she had her drawing pad with her and her colored pencils. She laid her head back against the headrest and told me she was staying in the car with Mike and sleeping there, too, but that I could go inside if I wanted.

I didn't know what to do. I wandered around for a little while looking for an old rusted toy car I had played with in the year before. I didn't see it. Then I went inside the house, stepping softly into the gloomy and creepy living room. It had no lights or windows, was shadowy and chilly even during the day, and was crammed with hulking pieces of dusty furniture. Looming over everything else was a lopsided grandfather clock whose booms woke us up at night, striking twelve no matter what the time. The wooden floors, covered by dirt-obscured Oriental rugs, sagged and creaked when I walked over them. On the right, I saw the steps leading to the top floor, which I'd never seen. The year before, I'd started up those stairs and could see the sky peeking through the roof. Halfway up, Peanut had blocked my way, "Don't go up there, Flower! There's bees up there!" I'd been stung by a bee before and was afraid of them so I stumbled back downstairs. Peanut never paid me much attention but she told me later, "When we sleep up there, there's a big ol' beehive hanging over the bed. We lay still so we don't make them mad." I felt itchy just hearing that. I wondered how those cousins could sleep peacefully with angry bees swarming over their heads.

On the left, I could see the sole bathroom with its blanketing shit odor. I hated using it and had only peed there, standing and quick, when I had no choice. I held everything else in. I'd die before I'd sit down over the rising sludgy puddle in that low, brown and crusted toilet bowl, always filled with unflushable floating stuff. I'd had to wipe my hands on my pedal pushers since there was never any toilet paper and you couldn't wash your hands because there was no running water.

I wandered into the kitchen. My grandmother was in there frying bacon on an old stove and Aunt Dolly and Sheena, my oldest cousin, were chopping it up. Grandma stood straight even while cooking. Her red-brown, sharp-cheeked face looked like the Indian on the nickel if he'd been facing forward. Her white braid hung down her back to her waist. Aunt Dolly's eyes, skin, teeth and even her nails were almost as yellow as hot dog mustard. My mother told me this was because Aunt Dolly had the wrong kind of blood when she had her second child, my cousin Number Two. Her doctors drained her and Number Two's blood and, replacing it with someone else's blood, which turned out to be tainted and made Aunt Dolly turn yellow with jaundice. She was the one relative on my father's side that Mother seemed to like. "It's too bad," Mother would say, shaking her head every time she told this story. "That blood they gave Dolly is gonna kill her someday." And it did. When I was ten, Dolly died of liver failure despite the fervent and unending prayers of her family and the faith healers they paid to pray for her.

I was terrified of Aunt Dolly's oldest son Herman but I loved her. She had a soft voice and a big smile when she looked at me. Mother said when I'd had measles I'd called for Aunt Dolly, no one else, in my fever. I hoped Mother was wrong about Aunt Dolly's blood and the horrible death she thought Dolly was facing.

I watched Aunt Dolly throw the bacon pieces into a bowl of steaming potatoes. Sheena started piling fried chicken on a plate. Then she noticed me. "Flower!" Sheena cried. Come on and give me and Grandma and Aunt Dolly a kiss! When did you all get here?" I was shy and gave them quick pecks. My grandmother's face was soft, under her cheekbones, and covered in flour. Sheena's blue eyes looked like marbles shot with silver sparkles and I could see small freckles sprinkled across her nose when I kissed her.

I said shyly, "Right now."

Grandma frowned and said, "Did Rachel come?"

"Mama's sitting in the car." I said.

I saw Grandma narrow her eyes and shoot looks at Aunt Dolly and Sheena.

"Why's she out there?" Grandma asked. She looked mad and I stood there, my mind working. I decided it would make them happy if I mentioned Dad. "Daddy's out there with Grandpa and them," I finally said. Grandma sighed, went back to fixing the food, curtly ordering me to go play piggy with my cousins until lunch was ready.

I leaped over the two broken wooden steps leading from the back porch and walked over to where my cousins were batting, throwing, spitting and cussing. All their eyes were on the ball or the bases. No one noticed me but I didn't care. I was timid around all my cousins but especially around Herman, who was crouching at one of the sandbag bases. He was a scruffy, mean, but always guffawing stick of a boy with a nickel-shaped head—flat on the back and front. He'd once twisted my arm while holding a pop gun to my head and I'd never forgotten it. He had two brothers—Stewie and Number Two-- so called because he was the middle brother and pooped a lot. Neither of them was as vicious as Herman but they cracked up laughing at whatever he did.

Herman spoiled any activity or fun we tried to have at The Farm or back in Chicago. When I was four, Aunt Dolly and Sheena took us cousins to Silver Beach, a nearby amusement park, to go on the rides. We kids were so excited we bounced up and down on the car seats the whole way. But then we went in the funhouse and Herman scared and pushed some little white kids. Suddenly, a lanky white man came to the door of the funhouse and shouted, "All you colored kids get out of here!"

Aunt Dolly and Sheena grabbed Herman, by the arm, laughing as usual, and dragged him to the car. They shoved the rest of us back in the car, too, and sped off. We never went to Silver Beach again.

This day, though, no one invited me to play piggy and I didn't know how anyway, so I moved over behind the batter, Jerri, cross-eyed and knobby kneed, to watch the game. Maybe I could figure out how to play if I watched closely. Right then, Jerri, a girl, swung the bat as hard as a boy. It hit me so hard above my eye, it felt and sounded like it split my head in two. I collapsed in the dirt screaming and crying. Blood started dripping out of my head and down the front of my dress. "Shit," I heard Herman say, "Where'd she come from?"

Sheena came running out of the house and picked me up and half-carried me into the house. Peanut followed: "Jerri didn't mean to. We didn't know she was there." When they led me into the house and the kitchen I sobbed loudly, chest heaving, my head raining blood, my nose running snot. When Grandma saw me, she asked my cousins, "Why did y'all let her stand so close to the bat?" She ordered Sheena to get the Musterole salve. My mother must have seen me get hit as she raced into the kitchen and asked me what happened. "I got hit with a bat," I said huffing tears and struggling for breath.

Mother asked my grandmother for some ice and a cloth to clean my head. Grandma said, "Rachel, we don't have any ice, we don't have running water yet. You know that. Y'all get me a towel and some of that water so we can wash the cut." She pointed at the scummy water that sat in an enamel tub on a side table for family wash-ups. Through my tears, I recognized and inwardly recoiled from that tub. The year before my grandmother had shown me that same bowl when I wanted to wash my hands. "We don't have any water inside. Grandpa and your dad are going to fix it but until then use that bowl to wash your hands." She had pointed at that same speckled enamel pot filled halfway with cloudy water.

Sheena rushed in with the Musterole, a strong-smelling yellow grease my grandmother used for every cut, bruise, scrape, or cough. My mother ignored the water in the enamel pot and cleaned my forehead with her saliva and spread some Musterole over it. The wound had stopped bleeding and was beginning to swell. My head pounded heavily and slowly like the hammer at the end of the Dragnet TV show.

I finally stopped crying and Mother walked me out to our car. My father came over to the car a few minutes later and looked in. "She all right?" he asked nodding his head at me. Mother replied flatly, "I want to leave this place early tomorrow, Ricky. I'll drive myself and the kids and you can come back with one of your brothers." "No I don't wanna do that." He shook his head and walked away.

I knew Mother hadn't wanted to come in the first place and after what happened to me was determined to leave early. My father was just as determined to stay and often ridiculed my mother's and other womens' driving. He almost never let her touch "his" car.

Later, Sheena came out with two plates for me and Mother piled high with crunchy chicken fried in bacon grease, potato salad with bacon and navy beans with a chunk of bacon fat floating on top.

Mother fed Mike from her plate and I dug into my food. When I finished eating, I felt better: my stomach was full and my head didn't throb as much.

Mother slept in the car that night although I can't say where Dad slept. Mike lay in her lap and she rested with her head back on the seat. I told her it made my head and neck hurt to sleep that way and so I wanted to sleep indoors. She said, "Watch out for that pee on those mattresses and don't sleep too close to those boys."

That night when I climbed onto one of the mattresses lined up on the gritty floor, I saw what Mother was complaining about. Right in the middle of the mattress was a dried yellow pee circle. The kids were expected to sleep on these pallets or in the beehive room upstairs. That night when the grown-ups turned out all the lights and I heard their loud snoring, I sneaked up and put on my robe so my legs wouldn't touch the "pee sun" on the sheet. I tried to close my eyes but the stains were all could think about so I knew I wouldn't get much sleep that night and I refused to get back in the car. *Why did I think it would be ok to sleep inside?*

Instead, I lay stiffly awake, smelling the toilet and remembering that it had been used that day by everybody in the house including Number Two. My sleep was restless and light in the struggle to keep my legs from touching the sheet while I pulled the thin blanket over my head to block the penetrating bathroom aroma. I rose the moment I heard a rooster crow at one of the farms nearby. I had watched Farmer Alfalfa cartoons on TV and knew how a rooster sounded. My head felt a little better despite the bad sleep. I dressed quickly and quietly. The cousins slept heavily and didn't awaken although I could hear sputtering bacon and eggs from the kitchen, my grandmother's heavy tread, and the murmuring of one of the aunts. I ran outside and up to our car. My mother was sitting up and feeding Mike something that looked like applesauce, which he ate silently. He was the quietest baby I'd ever seen, rarely crying, fretting or playing.

"Mama, there was dried pee on those mattresses like you said but I tried not to lie in it."

Mother nodded. "See, I told you not to sleep in there." She laid her hand on my head for a second. "How's your head?" Before I could answer, she instructed, "Flower, go tell your Daddy I want to go home." After my head got hit, after not sleeping well or being able to use the bathroom when I wanted and not having anyone to play with, I agreed with her and was very ready to go home.

I saw my grandfather Sam sitting on a stump while Daddy, and my uncles Mac, Andrew, Tad, Buzz, and Mickey, all short, bowlegged dark brown men, crouched around The Well, which was really just a big hole in the ground. Every time we visited, my grandfather, father and uncles sat in the front yard, drinking beer, while they stared into this big gaping hole. The Well was cavernous and had a deep and earthy funk--a combination of vegetation rot, animal and human waste, and musk. At its bottom was a maze of rusted and rotted pipes seemingly unconnected to one another. Every so often, Buzz or Mickey would jump down in the hole and hammer on the pipes as if that would somehow make them function. My father had solemnly explained to me that The Well controlled the indoor plumbing but was broken. When it got fixed, the toilet and faucets inside would finally work. He said Grandpa couldn't afford to hire a plumber but he and the uncles were going to fix it. My mother listened to that and laughed, "But none of y'all know how to fix anything so I'm not going to hold my breath."

She was right about that. I remember The Well was never fixed and water never flowed in that house. Between the awful odors of the house's toilet and The Well, all my memories of The Farm are enveloped in the smell of human waste.

That day, though, I tiptoed over to where Daddy sat gazing into the hole and told him Mother wanted to go home and that my head hurt. My grandfather and the uncles didn't even bother looking up at me, but then they never did. Dad didn't look at me either. "Tell her I said no." I stood there for a minute. *What could I do to change his mind? I'd hoped he'd want to leave.* Then I thought-- *uh oh, wait till I tell Mother what he said. There's going to be a fight.* I shivered at the thought of the oncoming storm. I ran back to the car and reported Dad's refusal to leave. "He's going to be sorry," was all she said.

Mother sat in the car staring unhappily at a picture of a house she had started drawing. The only times she had gotten out of the car were when I was hit by the bat and when she changed Mike's diaper on the hood of the car. I never saw her even go in the house to use the bathroom. She was determined not to talk or eat with Dad's family inside or outside. I could tell, though, Dad and his family didn't care whether she sat out there the entire visit. The throbbing in my head grew duller, but I was fidgety and anxious to go home, too, so I decided to stay by her side the whole day so I'd be ready to leave immediately. The situation momentarily improved when Aunt Dolly came out to our car, carefully balancing a plate of fried egg, bacon and mayonnaise sandwiches. I was hungry, ravenous, so I grabbed one and stuffed it in my mouth. Mother took hers stiffly but thanked Dolly. She opened her sandwich and fed bits of her egg to Mike.

I had eaten but I felt crazy with boredom—no one to play with, nothing to do. I wasn't welcome in the piggy sandlot, the kitchen or by The Well. My mother was getting more agitated by the minute, her foot tapping against the door, the ground. At one point, I kicked the other side of the car in sympathetic frustration as well. In the late afternoon, my father drained his beer bottle, threw it on the ground and came over to the car. "Get your stuff from the house," he ordered me, "and kiss Grandma goodbye." At last. I'd had enough of The Farm that day and maybe forever. I skipped through the door and dark living room, threw my pajamas and robe back in the paper bag we'd brought them in then ran into the kitchen clutching the bag. "Grandma, bye-bye. We're leaving." "Give me a hug and tell your daddy to come say goodbye" she said, her eyes sad and cast down as she spoke to me.

I jumped in the back seat and Dad took off, wheels spinning, looking furious. I tried to tell him that Grandma wanted to see him inside before we left, but he ignored me, and drove jerkily, his mouth turned down. I hadn't seen him go in the kitchen, speak to his mother, or carry Mike in to see her even once during the entire time we were there and I suspected that made Grandma unhappy. My mother's eyes were closed again, Mike was sitting on her lap, but looking at her set face, I knew she was angry, too. I braced myself for the inevitable fight, here in the car or at home, but I felt glad too-- at least we were leaving.

No one said a word until we were back on the highway. Then Mother announced, glaring straight ahead, "Ricky that's it. I'm never going to The Farm again. You can take the kids but I'm never going again." And she never did but then the marriage lasted only a couple of years more anyway. When my father forced me to return later on, I went kicking and screaming. The unchanging unsanitary condition at The Farm gradually came to completely overwhelm any good feelings I had ever had about being in the country and it made my flash crawl. I never developed any common interests or bonds with my relatives (they would have thought I was cracked if I asked them if they had enjoyed reading about the seven Chinese brothers who swallowed the sea or any other book, and I had begun to hate baseball) so it was dull as well. I usually sat in the car during the visits as my mother had, reading until time to return to Chicago. Then when I was twelve, I suffered a massive asthma attack while walking in the sand dunes that ran behind The Farm. After that, my father never bothered me to go again.

CHAPTER 1

67TH AND ST. LAWRENCE HORSEMEAT BURGERS

Although my mother refused to visit The Farm again after the trip when my head got busted, we still spent almost every Sunday with my father's parents. In 1956, in Chicago, my father had purchased a new car, a dark green Pontiac, with the orange Lucite Indian hood ornament, that he washed and waxed every weekend. When he parked the Pontiac, he carefully aligned it with the curb. "Look at that parking, Baby," he'd brag to me or my mother. "I can always get that Indian's nose to line up with the curb."

One Sunday in early spring that year, he parked in front of his parents' gloomy, brick building on the edge of all-black West Woodlawn on the southeast side of Chicago. I was almost seven, and my little brother Mike was almost four. My mother, who was pregnant, slowly climbed out of the car backwards, and waited until Dad was out of earshot. She warned me as usual not to ask to stay overnight or I'd end up sleeping on sheets that had been peed on repeatedly by my bedwetting cousins. My father, who had been born and raised on this block of spindly trees and worn but neatly-kept two flats and Victorians, crossed the street to talk to some old buddies who still lived in the neighborhood but he glanced over at us suspiciously. He could tell from Mother's crossed arms and whispering that there'd be a fight in getting her to visit nicely.

My mother slammed the car door and walked quickly up the cracked sidewalk, towards my grandparents' building, which was flanked by hard-packed, glass-studded dirt on both sides. The building had drooping, open front porches with a front stoop in the middle of two flowerless concrete urns with fractured sides. The back yard was my grandfather's personal junkyard where he kept disassembled old cars and toilets he had yanked out of buildings about to be torn down.

My brother dashed ahead, as he always did. I straggled behind clutching my favorite book—*The 500 Hats of Bartholomew Cubbins*. I carried it everywhere, had read it about fifty times especially whenever I felt anxious or bored. It was whimsical and funny and made me feel better if only for a moment. In fact, just heading toward this building made me uneasy. The vestibule was dark and cramped with its grimy mosaic inlaid walls and marble floor ringed by tiles so filthy you could not tell if they were black or dark green. The left wall was lined with broken mailboxes with unreadable and blurry penciled names. The odors were always the same: the chalky smell of dirty marble and bacon grease.

Directly in front of us was a wide door leading to the stairs to the first floor apartments where my grandparents lived. Glancing over my shoulder, I saw Dad yank Mother back before she could walk through the door and heard him warn her to be sweet to his parents even though he knew she hated them. Mother jerked her arm away—"Go to hell, Ricky. This visit better not take long."

As usual, I both shrank from and looked forward to this visit. I enjoyed my grandmother's cooking--a lot. And to my mother's continuing puzzlement, I liked looking at the old furniture and cut-glass in the living room that my grandmother called her "antiques" and Mother called "old junk". But, my uncles, all divorced or in transient relationships, dropped their kids, mostly males, at my grandparents' house on weekends and went to drink or play baseball with their friends. That meant that unhinged Herman was often around as he and his two brothers were often dumped at my grandparents'. During our last visit, Mike and I watched, sickened and cowering, as he tossed two frantically mewing and struggling kittens he had grabbed from their mother, into the building furnace's flames. He was doubled over with laughter the whole time. "Y'all better not tell Grandma or I'ma throw y'all in too," he had threatened us. After we saw what he had done, we ran upstairs and outdoors screaming and he ran after us, pelting us with dog poop he had scooped up in the alley. All the adults knew what he was like but never punished him. This day, the house was silent, though, with no cousins running around and fighting.

My brother ran and I walked down the tunnel of a hallway, past a yellowing old photo in a tarnished frame of my father and his brothers as boys. I passed the living room with my grandmother's prized Chinese jade room divider and saw the familiar rim of dirt around its bowing Chinese male and female figures. Mike barreled into the kitchen with its faded red and yellow linoleum and coil-top icebox and gave my grandmother, Ruby, a hard hug. I gave her a quick soft hug. No one ever hugged my grandfather, Sam Washington. Sam bounced hard in his chair, and shouted at me when he spotted me, "Hey you!" He never called me by name, didn't even really look at me, even though I was probably the only person who listened to the jumbled stories he told over and over. He was cackling and mumbling to himself as if picking up in the middle of a story he'd been telling for some time, "I jumped a moving train and smoked out of Sugar Cane, Louisiana because the Klan was after me. They don't like a proud colored man and I was prouder than them other fools. I'm a man, a proud man. Me and my sons walked into that store in Michigan and they called me 'uncle'! 'What you want, uncle,' them damn whites asked me. First I told them, 'I ain't nobody's damn uncle!' Then I said, 'Wait! Maybe I am your uncle! Maybe I am your uncle!' Ooh, them white folks hated that."

Grandpa looked the same as he always did --a squinty-eyed, rusty black fireplug, completely bald except for cottony tufts around the perimeter of his head, a cold cigar stub stuck in his mouth. He was sitting, as usual, in the dining room in a greasy armchair, wearing a stained and slack undershirt and pleated trousers. While he talked, he banged his fist on a heaven-sized harp, propped against his chair, tarnished and stringless, that someone unknown had abandoned at the house long ago. Daddy had disappeared. I had noticed he never seemed to spend much time with his parents during these visits although he insisted on making them. Mother didn't take off her coat or hat. She stomped past Grandpa without a glance. He grimaced, showing a few brown stubbed teeth. She stopped at the kitchen door. "Hello, Ruby" she said formally to my grandmother. "Hello, Rachel", my grandmother politely replied to my mother.

They faced each other and spoke without speaking.

Mother fled back to the living room. She always ended up there paging impatiently through the browned pages of the *Reader's Digest* volumes stacked on the coffee table. She never ate anything because she didn't think the food was clean and, therefore, nothing was offered to her. I stood at the kitchen door half-listening but unable to courteously escape Sam's familiar monologue. "I retired from the ice wagon business in '39 and ain't had to work a day since". "I'ma cut you niggers out of my will if y'all make me mad!"

Once Dad told me that Grandpa had a lot of money and he wanted his share when the old man died. Mother scoffed when I told her this, "Look at how your grandmother walks around in busted shoes and a used fur coat. She uses Crisco instead of cold cream on her face! Sam ain't got nothing to leave them!"

Sam rambled on to criticize my aunts, his sons' wives and girlfriends and how he told his sons to stop bringing tramps home. He never had anything good to say about any woman, especially my mother—"That gal thinks she's better than us but she ain't nothing but a nigger just like the rest of us. So all that education ain't gonna help her none." I hated to hear him talk bad about my mother when we visited. Mother had to know what he was saying: Dad had told her what Grandpa thought. I wondered why she didn't come out of the living room and tell him off like she told me and Dad she would behind Grandpa's back. "I don't think I'm better than him; I know I am, and my family is, too. Your mother puts up with him 'cause she's a doormat!" she'd say to Daddy and me.

Suddenly, Sam slumped and slept. Relieved that his story was over for that day, I sat in the kitchen where I could watch my grandmother working. Behind the kitchen, I could see the unheated wooden porch where Grandma's best friend, Aunt Carrie, slept most weekends. Aunt Carrie was a gangly, almost blind and childless widow who worked as a maid for a white woman on the north side during the week. Aunt Carrie wasn't around that day, though. I relaxed a bit while watching my grandmother cook. There was something soothing about seeing her shuffle around her cluttered kitchen. Ever since my mother told us she was going to have a baby, she fixed every meal quickly and threw it on our plates. We always knew what it was going to be: fried eggs and bacon or rice fried in bacon grease in the morning, peanut butter and jelly sandwiches at lunch, tuna casserole and green peas at dinner.

My mother might be a rushed and careless cook, but Grandma carefully and painstakingly measured and spooned together ingredients that I had never seen. That day, her long white braid hung limply as she hobbled between the stove and table in her faded housedress and the busted-front, easy-on-the-bunions slippers she wore everywhere. But then her "everywhere" was the dining room and kitchen. She seldom left the house except to go to The Farm. I asked Mother once why Grandma almost never left her house, even to go to church. Shaking her head as if the story was too pitiful for words, Mother said it was because Grandma's clothes were so raggedy that she had been too ashamed to go outside even when one her sons was struck and killed by a Coca-Cola truck. *Why didn't Grandpa buy her some new clothes with all the money he bragged about?* I wondered. I knew better than to ask that.

"You kids come on in," Grandma called to Mike and me. She paused as she never seemed to know what to say to us. "Herman and Number Two were here earlier and Sheena and them are coming later. Did you give Grandpa a hug?" We didn't answer or move. I was overjoyed not to see Herman and Number Two and didn't want to hug Grandpa, so I pretended I didn't hear her. My mind searched for something to say that would make her like me but all that ever came out of my mouth was something about food. I knew she disapproved of my mother and believed she saw me as her miniature version. I exasperated her. One time she asked, "Why don't you play with dolls like the other little girls? Put that book down!"

I'd hung my head without answering, her but thought *I'll never give up my books for a doll. Dolls are so boring! They just sit there.* I did care what she thought. But Grandma had so many grandchildren! It seemed to me that only the oldest and lightest-skinned granddaughters, like Sheena and her sisters, all a decade or more older than I, were real and dear to her.

I placed *Bartholomew* carefully down on a clean space on the table's oilcloth and hoped she wouldn't notice it. "Can I help?" I asked but she stuck her arm out like a crossing guard. "Don't touch anything!"

I asked her about two piles of brown powder sitting on a plate. "That's nutmeg" she said pointing to one, "and that's cinnamon." She lifted a half-filled pie crust-- "Lard makes the best pie crusts." I listened carefully and nodded. I'd try to remember. Maybe I could make a pie myself one day.

Occasionally, she'd hobble to the door and peek out at the TV. The picture on its fishbowl screen was so snowy and jumpy I couldn't tell what was on. She often peeked at the TV but never commented much except during the rare times when the screen was clear and a Negro entertainer such as Nat King Cole or Lena Horne was performing. "There's somebody colored on," she'd holler and everyone would come running to watch that Negro for his or her three minutes. Then she'd shuffle back to stir a pot of soupy navy or Great Northern beans or black-eye peas sprinkled with specks of salt pork which she served with every meal.

"I'm gonna fix y'all some burgers for lunch," she said. The burgers were unlike any I'd ever had. They were slider-sized, peppery, and served on Wonder Bread that had been steamed over a pan of water in the oven. The steaming made the bread even gummier and softer than normal and it stuck to the burgers like marshmallow.

My mother had ordered me many times not to eat these burgers: "Your grandmother gets that meat from that grocer on Eberhart. Everyone knows he's been selling horse meat to these fools since World War II. They wouldn't sell that stuff to anybody white and nobody white would eat it."

I didn't know or care whether the horsemeat story was true or not because these were the best burgers I had ever tasted, so good they didn't need relish, ketchup or mustard. Grandma plopped the navy beans down on our plates and poured glasses of red pop-aid --iced tea mixed with Kool-Aid. However, my heart sank when she handed us Grandpa's favorite desert--New York vanilla ice cream and vanilla wafers. Ugh! I hated vanilla wafers because they were so dry and tasteless and left them on my plate. I thought longingly of her birthday and holiday desserts: pound cake made from butter and lemons or coconut-lime layer cakes. Every Christmas and Thanksgiving she made cinnamon and nutmeg-laced apple and sweet potato pies.

"I'm fixing pot roast for dinner," Grandma promised after she served us the burgers. My heart lifted. Dinner would be good for a change. Grandma's fork-tender pot roast was wonderful, rimmed with a thin layer of fragrant fat and surrounded by sliced white potatoes. She usually baked a salt and honey ham to go with the beef, which she fried and made into sandwiches with mayonnaise and sweet potatoes. Later, she'd press the wax-paper wrapped, leftover beef and ham into our hands as we were leaving. Mother would frown but she'd let us take them.

After I ate, I ran to the living room where Mother was perched on the edge of a couch restlessly tapping her foot against the bottom of its brittle plastic slipcovers. When I ran in, she threw the Reader's Digest volume aside. "Ready to go?" she asked. I asked her if, before we had to leave, I could go play with one of my few friends--a boy about my age named Junior who lived in the basement apartment. "You know I don't want you going down there. Junior's father hits his mother and he might try to put his hands on little girls, too. Plus, he doesn't have a job." "Junior's daddy never says anything bad to me," I whined. Mother hesitated but then let me go.

I ran down to the basement apartment where Junior's plump, pretty mother was holding a piece of ice to her jaw as tears ran down her smooth, butter-colored cheeks. Junior's gaunt father sat barefoot, with eyes closed, in the dim apartment strumming an old guitar and muttering something that sounded like… "Lost my woman and.." I couldn't hear the rest. Junior was only too happy to escape outside, but he wasn't his usual self. He didn't want to play hide and seek or tag. He kicked the dirt, "I'm gonna kill Daddy," he said, throwing a clod of dirt against the building. "I wish I had a gun now. I can't stand him hitting Mama and Sister. I told him I was gonna do it, too. He don't believe me but I will."

I had heard my mother say more than once that Junior's mother ought to leave their father but that she stayed and took abuse because she didn't know how to do anything, not even housecleaning. My grandfather had grumbled that he didn't care if their daddy beat Junior and his mama's ass but that he was going to kick all their behinds out if they didn't start paying their rent on time. I asked Junior why they didn't just leave his father, but he said, with tears running down his face, that there wasn't any room for them with his mother's Mississippi family.

"You're it!" I yelled, finally prodding him into a game. I tagged him and ran. Suddenly, three of the bigger, tough boys in the neighborhood appeared and without warning punched Junior in the shoulder causing him to stagger. One with curly hair, uncombed and separated into beady "soldiers," shouted, "Boy, what you doing playing with girls?" Another, with snot dried in a white film under his nose hollered, "You a sissy, boy!"

The third, with a front tooth broken off at a sharp angle like a guillotine blade, chimed in, "We oughta kick yo' ass, man."

One of the boys tripped Junior so that he fell down backwards in the dirt. I stood there, hesitantly, expecting Junior to fight back. Still crying, Junior jumped up on his scabby knees but instead of attacking the boys who had tripped him, whirled and pushed me to the ground, twisting my arm behind my back. All the breath was knocked out of me. I was so winded I couldn't even scream, shout or twist myself out of his grip, and when I opened my mouth I could taste the glass-crusty dirt in my teeth.

"Punch that girl! Stomp her back!" the dried-snot boy urged Junior.

Then I heard the furious voice of my mother: "You little bastards leave her alone! Junior, you better tell your mother to come on out of that basement so I can tell her what you were doing!"

I heard feet pounding away into the distance as the three boys ran away. I rose and sat, then stood holding my head, trying to stop the throbbing. Junior stood staring at the ground. The building door creaked open and Junior's mother stood there, tears freshly streaming down her face, bandanna askew on her head, ruptured house shoes on her feet. My mother walked over to Junior's mother and stood hands on hips, feet wide apart, and shouted at her, "Do you know what he was doing? He knocked my daughter down and hit her. You better whip him 'cuz if you don't, I'm going to!"

Junior's mother stared at the ground, speechless, her tears falling on her bosom while my mother screamed at her. Then Mother ran over to me, grabbed me by my scraped elbow and dragged me into the building. I held my tears back. Lately, I avoided letting anyone see me cry, no matter how my body or mind might hurt, because other little girls did that and crying seemed too "girly" to me. I wanted to seem like a boy, tough, or like an adult, dignified, or at least stoic. I cried inside, though, because I couldn't understand why my friend Junior would do what he did.

CHAPTER 2

1916 WEST HUBBARD

Later that night, when we drove home on the Outer Drive by the glow of the globed streetlights lining the Drive, I could read the back of my mother's neck as if she was speaking: *"I never want my kids to visit that old, dirty rundown building again even though Ruby always wants to see them and Ricky. But she never steps in and tells those trifling tenants how to act. This isn't over."*

My father drove stiffly and silently, breaking into my thoughts only to order: "Kim, you and Mike look out the back window for Daddy and tell me if you see any police cars behind us." I knew the fight today with Junior was some kind of turning point in our lives although I was too young to say what. But I could tell it was a harbinger of bad things to come. I never saw Junior again and it was a long time before I saw those grandparents again as well.

After my parents' divorce, I visited them occasionally, awkward visits during which my grandfather steadily lambasted my mother, but these visits stopped abruptly when I was twelve, I don't remember why. I didn't see my grandmother after that until one day when I was about fifteen or sixteen. My mother and I had gone to the Goldblatt

Department Store basement looking for bargains and I was stunned to see my grandmother there standing straight in a faded housedress and broken shoes, white hair now bound around her head. She was accompanied by Sheena, still her faithful companion and probable driver. I'd heard from my father that Sheena had married a man who could pass for white and they and their children were living, undetected, in a white suburb. "Ruby," Mother said politely but coldly, "Your hair has gotten so white. I hardly knew you." "Rachel," Grandma said equally formally, "I just remarked to Sheena-- hasn't Rachel gotten stout?"

They stood there for few seconds glaring at each other and then, without glancing at or speaking directly to me, Grandma said, "Sometime, Rachel, would you let Flower come and see me?" Mother didn't reply and I hung my head. I never did go. I can't say why. Perhaps it was some addled teenage notion of loyalty to my mother. I never saw Grandma again and I'd heard my grandfather Sam had died before we saw her at that store (I didn't attend the funeral). She died when I was in law school. When I heard about her death, I felt ashamed for having ignored her all those years and alternately angry that my father had waited months to tell me she was gone. Ultimately, I accepted the fact that my ties to Grandma, weak as they were, weren't meant to last.

But I want to return to memories of the night where I got knocked down by Junior. Dad pulled up carefully in front of our building, looking over the side to make sure his white walls weren't touching the curb. I could tell from my parents' strained silence that a fight was coming. No matter what they fought about, I knew our flat building, as well as my father's family, were going to be central in the dispute. My mother hated our dilapidated building, with its tin Victorian ornamentation rusting along the front and sides of the building's roof and dangling precariously over the street. Its concrete stoop was fissured with crevices and crumbled edges caused by Chicago's hard winters and sweltering summers. The building was on Hubbard Street, on the near north side of Chicago (now trendy River North), which my mother insisted on calling the West Side and which she declared to be the bad side, hands down. "You got us living in a slum!" she shouted at Daddy on the day he moved us in. The building was sandwiched between two factories, one that made pies and one that bottled soda pop. Somebody had written "pussy" in big, white chalk letters and had tried to draw one on the outside brick of both factories.

The neighborhood was desolate, especially at night, since there were few street lights and the only traffic was rumbling pie and pop trucks. My family's four-flat building was the only true residence on the street. There were no trees or grass, and broken pop bottles lay everywhere. No birds sang and the only animals to be seen were solitary rats running from hidden place to hidden place or occasional stray dogs and cats.

When we stepped inside, Poochie, the Harris' skinny white dog with the bulging red-rimmed eyes snarled at us and lunged on his chain at my father. We all reared away from him. Poochie was always in the hall growling, pooping or scrambling in frustration on the floor and tugging at his chain which was looped tightly around the Harris' doorknob. He hadn't bitten anyone but he acted like he wanted to. "Them Harrises better get rid of that damn dog or I'm gonna do it for them," said Dad shying away from the dog. I liked the dogs in books but was afraid of Poochie. We climbed to our apartment, stopping at the hall toilet since we didn't have one in our flat. It had no light but was fairly clean, especially compared to the one the Harrises used. They left theirs dirty and Mother griped about the stink they made and the toilet paper they left on the floor.

Mother marched into the flat without saying a word and rushed us to bed. Mike always fell asleep immediately and stayed asleep, no matter what happened. I lay there, dreading the fight I knew was coming but fell asleep anyway. I was awakened abruptly by the sound of a plate crashing against the wall. There'd been fights like this before. Mother threw things and once my father got so angry he chased her shrieking down Hubbard Street with a junkyard gun Grandpa'd given him for protection. My heart beating like a drum solo, I'd raced over to Aunt Roxie's next door and begged her to help. Toothless and hunchbacked, Aunt Roxie, who claimed to be 100 years old and born a slave, tottered out on the street and shouted at my father, "Man, don't do this or I'm gonna call the police!" Aunt Roxie and everyone colored knew that the very mention of the police would quiet most Negro men down. Nothing was worth fighting about if it would bring Chicago's notoriously racist police down on your head and maybe land you in a casket.

In the next room now, Mother screamed, "I'm tired of the West Side, your goddamn parents in that filthy house, and that Farm. Every time we visit, something else happens. Flower might have been hurt or killed by those thugs and you just stood there!" I covered my ears and pulled the covers over my head but I could still hear every word.

My father was huffing with anger, "Rachel, your problem is that you think you're better than me and my family and you always have. I asked you to bear with me until I get on my feet. I just started a job at the Post Office but that ain't good enough for you. If the white man wants to give me a big-time job for kissing his ass like he did that nigger your sister's married to, then maybe I can do better."

I heard a few more bumps and crashes and then my mother hollered, "I'm putting you on notice. If you don't' find us somewhere to live on the South Side by next month this time, I'm going to my parents and taking the kids." There was silence then and I heard my parents' bedroom door close. I listened to the darkness for a while, heard the groan of the huge metal doors as they opened and closed for the pop trucks and, relieved, fell asleep again.

For a month or so after that there were no more fights, and the days took on a comforting rhythm. I ate grilled cheese sandwiches and tomato soup for lunch with Mike and Aunt Roxie, our baby sitter, and watched the Friday night fights with her as well. Aunt Roxie and I would punch the air along with the boxers, and sing "**Look** sharp and be sharp" the Gillette theme song. We were the first in the building to get a set and neighbors who didn't have one yet would knock on our door and stand around watching it in awe.

I attended nearby Talcott School on Ohio Street, which, contrary to the image and history of Chicago public schools of that era, was integrated. Whites (often the children of recent immigrants), blacks, Latinos and even a Hawaiian girl, all poor, attended. I don't remember any racial incidents and I loved my teacher, pixieish Miss Spiegel. Everyone seemed to take the diversity of the teaching staff and pupil population for granted.

After school and on weekends, I played Old Maid and Go Fish card games with my friend, Sharon, who was black and lived with her grandmother a couple of blocks over in a gargantuan building whose bricks were shedding and whose broken windows were stuffed with rags. The year before, when we were in kindergarten, Sharon and her grandmother had lived in a rickety frame building but it had burned to the ground in a fire so bad they had barely escaped. Sharon had been hurt in the fire and her skin still hung in singed strips from her arms. She was so wispy and weak in her one thin dress she was almost transparent but she was sweet and had a voice that squeaked like a Betsey Wetsey doll when you squeezed it. On the weekends, Mother would finally sit down with me and watch *Our Miss Brooks* and *The Honeymooners,* her favorite shows. It was the only time I heard her laugh. At that time, my father came home after I went to bed so I didn't see much of him. When he was home, my parents had stopped speaking to one another but at least they weren't fighting.

One morning in the spring, I woke up to find my mother holding a new baby boy. She'd given birth in the room next to mine but I hadn't heard a thing. I was amazed to see his tiny brown face peeking out of my mother's arms and surprised and disappointed to see he was not a she. "This is Eric, your baby brother," Mother said. "Where's Nicolette?" I asked. That was the name Mother and I had chosen for the new baby sister I wanted. It had never occurred to me the baby might be a boy. Mother shrugged as if to say "You get what you get." A few days after Eric was born, Mother woke me while it was still dark and told me to hurry and dress myself and Mike for a trip to Idlewild. My father was nowhere to be seen. She dragged a big suitcase with one hand towards the door while gripping the baby in her other arm. Outside, she pushed us into a waiting cab that took us to the downtown Chicago Greyhound Bus Station where she shoved us towards the escalator and onto the Michigan-bound bus.

CHAPTER 3
IDLEWILD, MICHIGAN SILVER QUEEN CORN

Idlewild, Michigan was where my mother's parents lived in a small cottage, in the woods, that my grandfather, Edgar Polk, had built with his own hands. We slept through the entire trip and when our bus stopped in the nearest town of Baldwin, we climbed off and saw my grandfather waiting. He called, "Rache! Kids!" and swung us down from the bus steps. The bus driver helped him heave the heavy suitcase out of the side compartment. Grandpa loaded everything and everyone into his dinged-up navy blue Pontiac and headed home. Edgar Polk was coffee brown, completely bald, barrel-chested, and short but taller than my other grandfather, Sam Washington. He wore farmer's overalls with a plaid flannel shirt layered over longjohns. His glasses were big, rimless, and had wavy glass thumbprints pressed into the bottom of the lenses to help him read. When he talked, you could see he had only one short tooth on each side of his mouth, like a puppy.

The car hit the highway and we passed forests broken only by small ramshackle cottages—"The Lily of the Valley," "Dun Roamin'," "Peaceful Petunia Cottage"--owned by Negroes who, barred from white resorts, came to Idlewild just for the summer and then went back to their homes in Detroit, Chicago, or Cleveland. My grandparents had spent family summers there in the 30's and then moved there permanently when my grandfather retired from the Post Office. Their house sat far back from the road at the end of a long driveway in a cleared place in some dusky and hushed woods. When we got to the house, my grandmother, Bertha, was in the yard hanging clothes on the clothesline. Bertha and Edgar lived simple lives in a stone cottage that, although small and lacking an indoor toilet, was trim and sturdily built. Behind the house was a garage which Edgar had also built, with a second floor apartment. We bumped our big brown and tan suitcase up the back steps into the cottage's tidy, unused parlor with its doily-topped rocking chairs. I ran into the kitchen and peeked out the side window, where I could see their outhouse. *Yuk! It was still there.* I had hoped they'd gotten an indoor toilet. In the summers before, we'd use the outhouse during the day and thunder jars-- portable enameled basins--at night. The outhouse crawled and buzzed with bees, wasps, flies and other bugs and crawlies. I itched the whole time I was in there. In winter, the bugs were gone but your bare butt froze.

The kitchen and dining rooms, large and wainscoted, were the center of their daily lives. The kitchen was dominated by a thunderously fiery pot-bellied stove used for cooking and living heat. There were hand pumps inside and outside the house for water. A television stood lonely and unused because there was no reception in the woods. A big cabinet radio didn't work either and crackled and spat when we tried to use it. The telephone worked but my grandfather didn't believe in paying for long-distance calls and no one called locally, so every night we sat around reading old blue-backed Nancy Drew mysteries by a kerosene lamp, working jigsaw puzzles, playing

Monopoly, listening to *Amos and Andy* or *Gunsmoke* on the surprisingly clear table radio or to my grandfather play honky-tonk piano.

My grandmother, Bertha, was a small, cold-natured, bespectacled, hair-bunned sparrow of a woman who was never still. She was not a hugger or a gabber. She cooked and baked all the time like my other grandmother but also quilted, crocheted, knitted, darned and sewed. When she wasn't knitting or cooking she worked in her flower garden with its sunflowers, bachelor's buttons, petunias, mums, and four o'clocks. My grandfather grew all the vegetables the family ate in an extensive garden: pole and runner beans, cucumbers, corn, tomatoes, watermelon, lettuce, cabbage, and collard, turnip and mustard greens.

The day we arrived, I sighed to myself as I watched my grandmother work without pausing. She always had a million chores laid out for us. Sure enough, after a brief greeting, she informed us we'd be picking fruit at some nearby farms all the next day. I remembered the last time we did that, the fruit was delicious: sugary red cherries, seed-filled but succulent blackberries, bursting navy blueberries, and cantaloupe-sized, sunset-colored peaches with juice as sweet and sticky as honey. But my back got tired and sore; those fields were treeless and the sun beat down on our heads. As the day wore on, bugs started biting. I dreaded spending a whole day there. I glanced over at my mother but she was smiling and nodding at Grandma's fruit-picking plan. I guess she was resigned to working hard during visits to her parents.

Throughout our time there, I don't recall ever really having a conversation with my grandmother. She didn't believe in conversing with or listening to children and spoke to my grandfather in fluent pig Latin so that we kids wouldn't know what they were talking about. While she worked, rather than talk to us, she whispered angrily to herself. The only time she spoke to me was to order me to do chores or accuse me of insolence when I said something she didn't like--which was all the time. I was generally too bewildered and timid to be fresh to adults, but if I asked why the sky was blue she'd snap "Stop being impertinent!" Or "Children should be seen and not heard," or if you seemed to be slacking—"Idle hands are the devil's workshop."

Every night we'd sit down to eat dinner. After farting loudly, Grandpa would solemnly boom lectures about table manners while we were eating, "Get those elbows off the table!," or he'd snatch away the book I was hiding under the table. He'd slap our hands if we reached for food rather than asking for it to be passed. "You're not in a boarding house!" or "That's a fork not a spoon—-stop shoveling!" He watched us constantly. The biggest sin: not keeping your shoelaces tied. Observing untied laces, he would warn, "Tie your shoelaces before you fall down and break out your eyeballs." I ate as quickly as I dared. Sometimes, though, Grandpa would tell stories mostly reminiscences about his Pullman porter days. His favorite tale was one about Robert Lincoln, the son of Abe. Robert was a nasty-tempered, rip-roaring bigot who called the porters "niggers" and even threw things at them. He rode the rails often and demanded constant attendance from the workers. "We spilled a lot of coffee on that buzzard 'accidentally'," Grandpa would hoot. "Sometimes, too much salt just fell in his food, 'accidentally.'"

Grandma didn't begrudge us food but she did start barking orders about chores early every morning. She'd forbid us to linger over breakfast or rest until our tasks were finished which they never seemed to be. To fortify and comfort myself before the long hard workdays I faced, I'd rush to the table every morning and gobble down rough-cut oatmeal mixed with stewed prunes, apricots and a butter pat and flooded with the heavy cream from the top of the milk bottle. Sundays were a bit slower. Grandma or my mother would fry bacon and we'd eat yeasty sweet rolls bursting with raspberry or plum jam from Jones' Bakery. Without fail, every day, Grandma fried hot water cornbread in flat shapes, called corn pones, on the wood-burning pot-bellied stove. We ate these crispy-on-the-outside, soft-on-the-inside patties slathered with salted, creamy almost white butter that came wrapped in butcher paper. She always had a pot on the stove with pole beans or turnip or mustard greens strewn with pork parts and new cut potatoes. Most of the vegetables we ate were as sweet as sugar—a sign they had grown under the sun. Every night, we had fire-engine red tomatoes almost as juicy and syrupy as peaches. At least once a week, we had Silver Queen corn on the cob, shucked and white, dripping with butter and salt and peppered so much, it left your hands looking like you'd played in dirt. There were canned pickles: green and yellow bread and butters with celery seeds and pickling spice drifting through the tangy pickle liquor, and dill slices caressed by floating dill weed and sugary, bumpy, but sometimes gritty, little gherkins.

Although Grandma had a serious case of insulin-dependent diabetes and squirted Sucaryl, artificial sugar, on her food during the week, she indulged herself on the weekend with desserts and baked goods. She baked: cobblers from the peaches and blackberries we gathered; flaky and meltingly soft baking powder biscuits with homemade cinnamon-swirled apple butter; and crumbly, hot oatmeal cookies scattered through with raisins like little moisture grenades. She never drank my Grandfather's beer, being a teetotaler, but instead made 12-lemon lemonade, or ground coffee beans and perked the coffee until it was robust enough to pump iron.

Despite the good food, our visit seemed like unending drudgery to me, although Mother didn't complain about the hard work. Perhaps she understood the currency for our staying there was this endless labor. Their simple life was hard work. On Mondays, Mother and I cranked the clothes wringer for Grandma, ran the hose into the washer and loaded it, scrubbed underwear on a washboard, and hung clothes to dry. We heated heavy irons on the top of the stove and ironed and folded the laundry on Tuesdays. On Wednesdays, we swept the wood floors and hung and beat the living room's hand-hooked rugs. We spent Thursdays weeding flower beds, picking, snapping and shucking vegetables such as corn and pole beans, and pouring scalding water down molehills. Fridays, Grandma cooked and baked for the week and each day we washed and dried dishes. Sundays we went to the Methodist church.

The services were wordy and dull except for those Sundays, when Madame Braxton performed. She was a 6'3" woman who was rumored on the church grapevine to actually be a man. Heavily rouged, powdered, and wigged, often in a glittering evening gown or wrapped in a mink stole, Braxton had a bracing bass voice, and one song—*In The Garden* which she sang eagerly and vigorously. I wanted badly to giggle while she sang and knew that would get me a whipping, but listening to her was transfixing--not because she was so talented but because we'd never seen anyone like her. After the service, my grandmother would stay and meet with her garden club friends or other retired Chicago transplants while my brothers and I squirmed restlessly on the back pews. My mother waited more patiently. My grandfather wasn't there to be tortured—he refused to attend.

Every Saturday, the whole family would pile into the back seat and drive into Baldwin or Reed City to visit my grandparents' doctors, and buy milk, butter, salt pork, whole chickens, and unsliced bologna. We'd always stop for butter-crust bakery bread bursting with yeast and sweet rolls at Jones Bakery and Ice Cream Parlor. Jones' ice cream was so pure and rich, the smell of heavy cream and vanilla hung like a fragrant cumulus in the store's air.

Then because Grandma liked to throw salt pork or ham hocks in our nightly greens and pole beans and fry pork chops, about once a month we'd go to Mother Blake's. Mother Blake was an ancient, sun-darkened and hunched woman who lived in a decrepit witch's hut and kept a brace of smelly hogs for slaughter. Grandma would call out, "What you got?" to Mother Blake and the old lady would point to her hogs snorting in the brown mud in their pens. I avoided looking at the pigs, whose hairy jowls and snotty noses were disgusting. If I looked at them too long, I wouldn't be able to eat or enjoy the pork chops we brought home. I'd run back to the car when Mother Blake got ready to kill Grandma's pick. I didn't want to see anything die, not even those nasty pigs. Once, though, I didn't get away quickly enough. Grandma chose a good-looking pig, one of the cleaner ones, and Mother Blake whacked him on the head with a giant axe, quickly sliced off some ribs and chops and side meat, dropped them in a salt water tub to wash off the blood and some of the mud, then scooped them into a brown paper sack. She'd also hack off ears, snouts, tails, or feet if that was what you had a taste for. If my grandfather was along, we'd stop at Jax's, a cinderblock highway roadhouse for a quart bottle of Pabst Blue Ribbon, his nightly treat. In the evening, he salted his beer or buttermilk (even though his kidneys were failing), cut off a slice of limburger cheese, slapped it on a saltine, and leaned back to listen to *Amos and Andy* or *The Lone Ranger* on the radio. Sometimes we joined him, eating crimson and emerald watermelon that he salted and peppered for us like his beer although Grandma tried to stop my brothers from eating watermelon at night. Eating watermelon or drinking pop at night was thought to make boys pee in the bed. She also was reluctant to feed us peaches as their juice was said to make permanent, unwashable stains on clothes.

That summer was lonely, though. Whether I was working on those chores, eating or sneaking a peek at a book, I was lonely. No children lived nearby and Grandma's friends' grandchildren didn't live in Idlewild. My only solace was in food. When I watched Grandma prepare food or ate it, I didn't feel so lonely because I was doing something that I actually liked. Eating a plate of string beans with new potatoes, I didn't worry so much about what was going to happen to us and where we were going to live.

We didn't hear from my father and I didn't miss him, if only because when he wasn't with us, there were no fights, no tension, no throwing or guns. I did endless chores, read books when I could and watched Grandma cook. Sometimes, I sneaked off from the chores and walked around the woods and along the deserted roads near the cottage looking for run-over snakes, or "runners" as Grandpa called them. I was curious to see a snake up close even if dead. He claimed the dead bodies were everywhere but I never saw one or any wild animal dead or alive, no cars and no people. The air was so still you could hear bees hum and smell the sweet hay scent of sun-dry weeds by the road. I'd pick and chew the carroty-tasting Queen Anne's Lace that grew abundantly by the road's edge and walk past Dr. Nelson's green-shuttered mansion set far back from the road on an open field. I never saw the doctor and wondered if he was imaginary since no one had ever seen him or knew anything about him but his name. The house was quiet and looked abandoned, but there was always a gleaming Cadillac parked outside.

Back at the cottage, this grandmother, like the other, was distant and impatient with me. She'd snap "Stop reading and wash those dishes!" or if I went in the bathroom (they finally got one indoors), she'd holler, "I know you've got a book in there! Come out and get to work!" If she noticed me watching her cook, she didn't let on, ask for help, or offer to teach me, although I'd have been willing. Cooking was the only household task that interested me and the only one for which she didn't want my assistance.

That summer, Mother prowled restlessly about the cottage, nervously but absently doing chores and tending to the baby. At least twice each day I'd hear, "He bought a new car and I ended up having this last baby at home like a slave. We couldn't even afford County Hospital! I'm gonna finalize my divorce and never see that bastard Ricky again!"

I believe my mother's continuous fussing was the result of her perpetual frustration with her life. Her fretting became the soundtrack of the twenty-one years I lived at home. Even after their divorce, she fussed about: her short, homely, low-wage earning, car-buying, baseball-playing ex-husband. Then there were her three lazy, messy kids—me and my brothers, and our painful and unwelcome births; her poorly paying substitute teaching jobs with disobedient children; the iffy neighborhoods we lived in; Chicago's three cold seasons; her woes as an ugly duckling middle child; her still-born art career; her ailments—-asthma and female troubles; and, sometimes, the "white man's foot on our necks." She could talk for hours on the meanness and racism of Mayor Richard J. Daley alone. Most of all there was seething about the lack of money—-all conversations, pleasant or otherwise, led to a discussion of our ongoing, unchanging poverty and inability to afford just about everything.

While we lived with them in Michigan that summer, her parents offered little advice and little reaction to her agonizing. Grandpa wearily remarked once in response to one of her angry tirades, "Ricky's no good, you were right to leave."

Despite their presumed silent sympathy, I sensed they were secretly impatient for us to move on. I worried—-*Where will we go if they kick us out?* And even though Mother worried out loud to them about her troubles, she didn't talk to me about what would become of us. She didn't notice I read *Bartholomew Cubbins and the Ooblek* over and over, or that I walked the woods and roads alone or with Mike when I wasn't doing chores. I couldn't stand the silence on this issue so I asked her, "Mama, when will we go back to Chicago?" She'd only say that was for her to worry about. Unsatisfied and uneasy, I lay awake every night in anxiety. *Would we have to go back to Hubbard Street? Would we have nowhere to live?*

Mother whined and jittered, I stewed, Mike dug in the backyard dirt or followed me around and Eric cried. I knew my grandparents were sick. My grandmother shot herself in the leg with a huge needle every morning for her diabetes and my grandfather's kidneys and heart were giving out. Under his long-johns, he wore a thin rubber bag visibly full of bloody urine and at least once a week he had sudden and lengthy nose bleeds. He moved as if his shoes were weighted, and he'd become almost skeletal since we moved in. I realize now he was only about sixty-five but he looked ancient to me. One afternoon, I was helping him weed his garden when he said, "I'm not going to make it. I wish I was." He stared into the woods just beyond the garden, and from where I kneeled I could see a milky film covering his eyes that I'd never noticed before. My stomach churned and I started pulling weeds out right and left. *What would happen to us if Grandpa died?* I wondered. *I liked him better than Grandma. Would she let us stay? Would she care what happened to us?*

Mother seemed oblivious to the uncertainty of our situation. Then, one day Dad appeared, unshaven, alone, wild-eyed. He pulled up in the green Pontiac, now the dirty green Pontiac. He jumped out and started arguing at the top of his voice with Mother, who was standing with me hanging wash outside the cottage. Mike was at our feet shoveling dirt into anthills. That old feeling swept over me. *Run! Hide!*

Dad was shouting and waving his arms around frantically. "You took my kids! You took Mike! I didn't know where you were! Now you're talking about divorce! What about what I want?" Dad yelled.

"If you had acted like a man this never would have happened," Mother yelled back, hands on hips, head tilted back, legs wide apart. "I told you I was going to leave but I guess you didn't believe me. Now you're here hollering about Mike like he's the only child you got. What about Flower and Eric?"

My father blinked and mumbled something about not really knowing the baby, Eric. *What about me?* I wondered. Grandpa limped slowly forward from the garage where he'd been working and jumped in, "Rache told me about you, Ricky. You're no good. You better get on out of here and go on back to the city."

My father roared, "I am not no good!"

Then, suddenly, Dad grabbed Mike, leaped in the car and sped off. I collapsed in the dirt screaming and crying, the wind knocked out of me. My world instantly turned upside down. Mother and Grandpa jumped just as quickly into the Pontiac and sped off in pursuit. That night, my grandmother and I ate corn pones and runner beans in sad silence. This was one time food didn't comfort me. My grandmother, never very sympathetic, said only, "They'll get Mike back." I couldn't respond. I felt lifeless. I rarely cried but this snatching of my little sidekick felt like the end of the world to me.

For three days, Grandma and I heard nothing. We went about the chores and tended to Eric silently. Then, coming up the drive I spotted the dusty Pontiac. carrying Mother, my grandfather and Mike. Mike was so dirty he looked scorched and his braids stuck up as if they were wired. Waves of joy and relief flooded my body. According to my mother, they had no trouble finding him. He was playing outside my other grandparents' house in the glassy dirt with another child from next door.

This episode seemed to wake Mother up. She was going to have to get on with the divorce and start a new life with us. So, after she brought Mike back, Mother left Michigan. She bought an old car, drove back to Chicago and stayed away about four months. I didn't know where she was. She didn't call me and my grandparents wouldn't say where she was. We just understood we were to stay with them and wait for further developments. Boy, did I miss her.

When the school year started, I rode the bus with the other children to the all-black, one-room schoolhouse in Yates Township. The Township's kids were even poorer than the children at my school back in Chicago. According to my grandmother, since there were no jobs in the area, most people were on "relief". All the grades were in one big brown-painted room. At lunch, I'd open a bologna or peanut butter sandwich with a piece of fruit and see kids who brought just one piece of Wonder Bread smeared with margarine or jelly. We rode a school bus to and from our homes, and I was surprised when two of the boys disappeared under a tarpaper-covered hole in the ground. "That's where they live." explained Adeline Springfield, a bony little bird of a girl who rode next to me most days and whose raggedy clothes were held together by safety pins.

The older kids at Yates were rough and roamed the small playground in clusters beating up and threatening smaller kids. "Is it true you read like a sixth grader?" I was asked by one of the bigger boys wearing a dirty white shirt that was too small for him and hiked up over his stomach. Before I could answer, he yanked my braids and shoved me to the ground.

The one teacher for the entire school, Mrs. Johnson, a kind woman who liked me, had told the class that although I was in the second grade, I read on the sixth grade level. Mrs. Johnson was pregnant and after the baby was born, she dropped by my grandparents' house. Peeping around the door to the living room, I saw Mrs. Johnson proudly announce to Grandma that she had named her new baby girl "Kim". "Mrs. Polk, I just hope she'll be as smart as your granddaughter. By the way where is Kim? I came over because I wanted to tell her in person," Mrs. Johnson said looking around the room. My grandmother called me and I came out of my hiding place, with head hanging. I mumbled "Thank you" and then ran and hid.

I'd never been singled out for much positive attention before, and for some reason it made me feel uncomfortable and even ashamed. Grandma was incensed at me. She called Mother in Chicago and demanded that she punish me for ingratitude. "Someone liked her name enough to name their baby after her and she just stood there and then hid when that woman came by. Rachel, that girl needs a whipping!" My mother didn't whip or scold me but she didn't acknowledge or even mention the honor or my behavior either. The subject was closed after that.

The months dragged on in Idlewild. Mother was still gone. The school bus I rode dropped me off on Highway 10 every afternoon and I'd walk the half mile or so to the cottage. One day, as I jumped off the bus, a hound dog darted out of the woods next to the highway and the bus driver ran over him and killed him. The dog's dying yelp was bloodcurdling, blood and guts flew all over the road and I became hysterical. I couldn't stop crying as I ran home. I kept seeing that poor dog and pieces of him up and down that side of the highway. I was still screaming and crying as I told Grandma what happened. She snapped, "Stop that crying right now! It's only a dog."

Shortly thereafter, Grandma exiled my brothers, four and six months, and me to the unheated, locked-from-the-outside garage apartment during the night. We had blankets but it was so cold, we shivered through the night and I'm amazed we didn't get sick. Eric would dirty his diapers and I never knew what to do. I was too small to even lift him. Grandpa would trudge upstairs in the morning, unlock the door, let us out and carry Eric and Mike indoors. I'd dress by the stove but never felt warm. I had just turned seven and thought being stuck in the garage was a punishment for my apparent ingratitude to Mrs. Johnson when she named her baby after me or because I cried about the stray dog that got killed.

After awhile, I concluded she stuck us up there because we were annoying--Eric cried a lot, as babies do, and she didn't want the bother and the noise of any of us. One day my mother returned as suddenly as she had disappeared, her divorce finalized. Neither Grandma nor my grandfather admitted they had locked us in the garage at night and I never told my mother about it. I was just glad to see her and was ready to leave.

CHAPTER 4
3806 S. ELLIS

Mother bundled all our belongings into a green on green '49 Pontiac she'd bought and we left Michigan for a new apartment on 38th and Ellis in the all black Lake Park neighborhood on the near South Side in Chicago. The Lake Park neighborhood curved around Lake Michigan between the south 30's and 40's. Our block on Ellis was lined on both sides with once-glorious but by then battered Victorian and Edwardian two, four and eight flats, the lineup broken by the occasional dilapidated frame house. I was glad to get back to Chicago. I had had enough of the lonely countryside, my rock-ribbed grandparents, their grueling task-focused life and that bleak one-room school. It felt good to see kids and adults who weren't family members walking around, riding bikes, jumping rope, watching TV, going to the movies and parks, and having fun. It was wonderful to be able to visit the library and the YMCA. I even took acting lessons and appeared in a play at the Washington Park Fieldhouse. Our new apartment was in a gigantic and gloomy gray stone Victorian building with a grand central staircase with a mahogany balustrade. Our apartment was spacious but drab and drafty. Mother fussed less about what a dud Daddy supposedly had been and started drawing again—always a sign she was happy. "I'm glad we got away from Ricky," she would say as she danced a clumsy happy-dance around the kitchen or living room. "He kept us in a pickle buying all those cars. Our future's going to be a lot brighter without him around." She even vowed cheerfully to start sketching our pictures annually so she'd have a self-made record of our changing appearances.

Mother substitute taught all day at an elementary school, Howland, on Spaulding Street, in the North Lawndale neighborhood on the West Side and took Mike with her for kindergarten. North Lawndale had long been a neighborhood of working-class Central and Eastern European immigrants but they were fleeing the neighborhood as even poorer blacks rapidly streamed up from the south to work in factories and industrial sites like Sears and Western Electric.

Eric stayed with a sunny-natured and warm Jamaican woman who lived across the street on Ellis, Mrs. Dye, and I'd walk to and from Oakenwald Elementary School and let myself in at home most afternoons with a latch key. Some days, however, I'd sit around Mrs. Dye's house reading the only children's book she owned—a dog-eared copy of *Farmer Boy* by Laura Ingalls Wilder. Well, actually, I spent the time salivating over the descriptions in the book of the meals eaten by her prairie family. As I waited for my mother, Mrs. Dye sometimes fed me her delicious coconut, beans and rice pilaf or her coconut and pineapple cake.

I wasn't so sure if I liked the Ellis apartment or not. While it was roomier than our Hubbard flat, there were other problems for me to worry about. One was Mother's new-found friend, Mr. West. Another was my parent's on-going, sometimes physical, post-divorce war and still another was my new school, which promised to be even rougher than Yates Township.

We first met Mr. West when we joined a nearby newly sprung neighborhood church, Jesus is King, pastored by a young progressive preacher, Pastor Garrett. Tall, ebony-skinned and very young,

Pastor Garrett enthusiastically welcomed us into the congregation. We immediately liked Garrett, who seemed to be a pleasant and relaxed contrast to the elderly sing-songing and shouting pastors at the churches we had irregularly attended in the past. I had turned eight, and we started attending most Sundays because we found the music, rituals, and the fellowship of the parishioners to be comforting. One Sunday, Pastor introduced Mr. West, "I want you all to welcome Mr. Joe West," Pastor Garrett announced drawing West forward. "He's going to be a great new usher and church member." The ushers were a clean cut crew--short-haired, smoothly groomed. Carrying the collection plates, they marched straight as soldiers in v-neck sweaters, slacks and buttoned down white oxford shirts with striped ties. However, the new usher, Joe West, wore a dingy checkered suit jacket with sleeves that drooped over his hands, cotton khaki pants that didn't meet the tops of his grimy socks, and a grayed white shirt.

During the introduction, an old lady loud-whispered in the pew behind me—"I heard he's crazy." I looked around and she smiled at me and shook her head in pity. West didn't look crazy but his long and nappy hair, unheard of in the 50's, made me giggle. His natural hair was not thundercloud-shaped like a 1960's or 1970's black-power Afro but just looked like he couldn't afford a barber. No matter how poor you were, in my 1958 Chicago world, you fled from nappy hair by cutting, suppressing and managing it with grease and heat. West smiled at the congregation showing long and loose teeth that drifted on his lips like wobbly planks.

My family politely shook hands with West after the service. We were walking home when my oldest brother noticed the new usher shuffling along a few feet behind us and pointed him out. My mother shrugged. "Maybe he lives over this way." But, the next thing I knew, West had gotten a job at the Post Office and was visiting every night after work. He'd sit across from Mother, she dozing after her long day teaching, and look earnestly in her eyes if she were awake.

The Chit'lin Coast

His mumbled monologue was always the same. "Rachel, you're in a trance. I want to tell you what the woman is saying to me. What she is saying in my head." He'd repeat this statement to my nodding and sleeping mother while stamping his feet and banging his fist on his chair's armrests to wake her up. I never saw Mother totally awake in his presence. Night after night, at about 10:00 p.m., our mother would go to bed—-by herself. West would remain in the chair muttering and talking to the woman in his head. At some point, he would get up and leave.

I was disgusted and frustrated with Mr. West for he was taking our mother's attention I thought we should have. After our long sojourn in Idlewild and sad separation from Mother, I yearned for her time and couldn't figure out why she let him hang around. He looked bad and talked crazy. I wasn't sure what the words "trance" or "you're insane" meant but I knew West had been in a "nuthouse" in the past and I thought I knew what that meant. "I feel bad for him and y'all should be a little nicer. He's been through a lot.", Mother would say when we complained about his nightly visits. Mother explained that she felt sorry for him and was helping him because his dead wife had driven him bats. Supposedly, the wife had foolishly and recklessly insisted that their daughters attend private schools, take ballet and piano lessons and generally live the lives of doctors' daughters, even though West was a social worker with a miniscule salary and his wife a poorly paid teacher. Both tried to keep up by working those jobs as well as other part-time jobs, giving the wife a severe and ultimately fatal case of diabetes and catapulting West into a permanent mental breakdown.

Mother never mentioned what I had overheard him tell her--that his daughters, now grown, would have nothing to do with him. Their mother's death and his subsequent breakdown humiliated them and, worse, forced them out of their comfortable home and school life. They ended up being raised by their grandmother in a dicey neighborhood and were removed from the fancy schools.

My brothers and I listened to Mother's explanations about West's unhappy life but it was her own behavior we couldn't understand. Mother was having enough trouble taking care of us. Why did she even give him the time of day? To us, a person's nutty or erratic behavior was caused by an evil(disagreeable) disposition, an empty wallet, mean relatives or cruel bosses. Most folks in our community believed there was nothing you could do about "craziness" unless the person became violent, and then you had them committed to a "nuthouse". "Mental illness" was considered to be a term and condition relevant only to whites and which only they were financially able or willing to treat.

Then, West disappeared, only to reappear two weeks later. He gravely explained that he'd been attacked and robbed while walking and talking to the woman in his head in Washington Park late one night. As he had only had a dollar, the robber got angry and slugged him in the head with an iron bar. West wound up in the local charity hospital where they inserted a metal plate in his head to protect the wound, which he willingly showed us.

After the attack, West hung around even more often and whatever slight sympathy we had for him quickly faded. Just the sight of him made me want to tear my hair out. "I thought Mama would be tired of him by now," I groused to Mike. "But since he got hit in the head, she feels even sorrier for him." Then he disappeared again. I held my breath hoping it was permanent. We never knew what happened. Mother didn't mention him and I was just relieved he wasn't around. I didn't know then, though, that we hadn't seen the last of West.

Mother dated sporadically after that. There was gap-toothed Mr. Spurlock, who sold Fuller brushes and women's nylons door to door. Then there was a dope-smoking fellow teacher, Mr. Radford, a Jamaican who dated all the single female teachers at Howland at least once.

Other than that, she didn't go out much. She was prematurely gray, had three kids, and talked about her divorce and bills to anyone who'd listen. Even so, Dad would suddenly appear at odd times—after school, Saturday mornings, whenever, and start fights with Mother about her so-called dates. They fought about what man she might be seeing, how Dad suspected she might be spending the monthly $60 child support payment on herself, and who should have custody of Mike. I dreaded seeing him because it meant a fight was about to start. At first, the fights were just shouting matches, which upset me a lot, but later they became physical, which terrified me. One afternoon he showed up and they each grabbed Mike by an arm, pulling like they were trying to split him in two. Suddenly, Dad hauled off and socked Mother in the face. I grabbed a broom and started whacking him with it. Tears ran down my face while I beat Dad's head with a broom taller than myself not just because Mother and Mike were shrieking and crying but because I was so sick of it all—the fighting and arguing, the fixation on Mike, the unending hostilities over nothing. The broomstick incident seemed to get Dad's attention because after that my parents' arguments never became physical again, at least not while I was around.

CHAPTER 5

MORE ELLIS

In 1957, we were still living on 38th and Ellis. I ran home from second grade one afternoon and breathlessly announced to my mother, "Mama, the other kids said that a bad boy found a big stick that had nails all up and down it, and he hit Miss Armstrong, my teacher, in her head." I explained that when the teacher came back to school after the attack some kids said you could see a metal plate, like Mr. West's, in her head. The boy who hit her had been kicked out of school.

The attack on my teacher, was the most electrifying and scary thing that had happened at my public school, Oakenwald, since our move back to Chicago. Oakenwald was a small smoky-yellow brick school located near the railroad tracks with a breathtaking view of the Outer Drive and Lake Michigan. Miss Armstrong was the tallest female teacher, robust and stern. She usually wore an iron-gray shoulder-padded suit, with her hair skinned back in a doughnut-shaped bun.

I hiccupped out what little I knew about the event. Mother stood at the stove in the overcoat she wore inside and outside our apartment, stirring soup, surrounded by the chilly and oily blue smoke, belched out continuously by the clanging but ineffective coal-burning furnace in our basement. The smoke seeped around the front door and through the cracks in the wall. She frowned but said nothing. I knew she didn't like my school. The kids were tough--I had my lunch quarter snatched twice by larger girls. One hulking girl, surrounded by her friends, had threatened me: "I'm gonna beat your butt at 3:00!" Shirley Atkinson, a girl I walked with to school most days had warned me, "Uh oh, girl! She'll pull your bra off if you fight her and rip your pierced earrings out of your ears." My ears weren't pierced and I barely knew what a bra was but my knees knocked with fear. *What had I done to bring this on?* For at least a month, I slipped out a side door and took a different route home to avoid that girl. When I'd told that story to my mother she'd looked thoughtful but said nothing.

Then one day, I was walking home with Shirley and I almost stepped on an enormous dead rat. He was bloated, his intestines grotesquely festering and oozing, his fur partially bald in places. Shirley's big brother William, a school crossing guard, heard me screeching. He ran over and said, "Little girl, I'll get rid of him." He picked up the dead rat by the tail and slung him into some bushes. During the swing, some of the rat goo got on my sweater, and I ran home hollering even louder while desperately trying to wipe it off. I felt contaminated and despite two hard-scrubbing baths that night still didn't feel clean. This was one of the many dead rat carcasses (often freakishly white or skinless) lying on the sidewalks along the way to school. I'd tell Mother about them and she'd grimace and slam her cooking pots on the stove but didn't comment. However, when she heard the story about Mrs. Armstrong, she said, "I'm worried about you going to that school." She asked only one question that could be considered suspicious about the authenticity and details of the attack: "Didn't you tell me Miss Armstrong was over six feet tall? If she's that tall, how could a second grader go upside her head?"

One day I was hopping with more news: "Mama, Miss Armstrong is leaving. She says she doesn't want to teach colored kids anymore because colored kids are so bad." Mother said, "Well, she's white isn't she? I'm not surprised. She probably didn't want to teach there to begin with."

At the beginning of summer vacation, Mother announced she was sending me to another school, recommended by Pastor Garrett, called St. Matthew's, in the fall. I wasn't sorry to leave Oakenwald as I can't now remember learning anything at that school. I sat at the back of the classroom quietly where I was never noticed or called on by Miss Armstrong. We took a lot of true/false and multiple-choice tests but no one ever told us how well or poorly we did on them. No one seemed to care. Mother wanted me to go to a better school in a better neighborhood, even if I had to travel across the city to do it. I felt any school would be better than Oakenwald.

I've always believed that Mother's transferring me to a private school was also fueled by her futile and unacknowledged competition with her sisters, who'd married men she thought were better providers, husbands and fathers than my own. Mother was convinced she'd been born behind the eight ball. She was a middle child and thus, according to her, ignored by her parents; a self-proclaimed ugly duckling compared to her impossibly beautiful sisters; had married completely out of desperation and bore more children—three--than her sisters. She also felt my father measured up poorly to her own father, whose thrifty and hard-working ways were her idea of male perfection. She'd say countless times: "My sisters married men who take care of them. I married Ricky and had all these kids and all he did was buy cars. He was no good." She'd cross her arms and frown, "They all live in houses their husbands bought out in the '80's and '90's," referring to the then most desirable neighborhoods on the far South Side for upwardly mobile blacks. Her sisters' children were enrolled in Catholic schools with other middle

The Chit'lin Coast

class black children. Mother couldn't rest until she found a private or parochial school for me that she could afford on her meager salary. The day she made the decision to transfer me(Mike attended the school where she taught and Eric still wasn't in school), she told me, eyes sparkling with triumph, "Now my daughter's going to go to a private school, too!"

By then we were moving again anyway. The official reason was because the building and street were being demolished to make way for the Robert Taylor Homes and Stateway Gardens housing projects--Chicago's idea of progress. We were glad to leave Ellis, though, with its vermin-welcoming environment and hard living. During our first winter there, my mother's parents stayed with us to escape their even more severe Michigan winters and to be closer to their other two daughters and son and to be near better doctors. Grandpa, arms waving, seemed to enjoy describing how he could look across the gangway at the building next door at night and see dozens of rats swinging from the curtains and dropping like paratroopers onto the garbage can lids below. He'd hoot, "My God! Those rats was partying up a storm!" My grandmother and mother turned away or bolted from the room in disgust when he told that story. I felt queasy and anxious, although I hadn't seen any rats in our apartment. My skin chilled at the thought of them. Grandpa's stories made me shudder and think of the rat goo incident. I made sure I never looked out his bedroom window at any time. The roaches were no joke either. We'd complain to the landlord and he'd send Mr. Berry, the exterminator, a tan gnome of a man who'd shuffle around our apartment and squirt some foul-smelling stuff in the corners. But the roaches seemed to lap that glop up like soda pop.

Also, our apartment was always nippy. Although the building's rumbling furnace choked out black smoke that kept everyone coughing, it emitted little heat. We wore our coats in the house all fall, winter and spring. Finally, whether it was caused by that smoke or a large moldy rug rolled up in my bedroom, one morning I woke up gasping for breath. I felt as if I was being smothered, and the doctor, who visited our apartment to treat me, admonished Mother, "Ma'am your apartment is too smoky. This girl has asthma. Get her out of here."

CHAPTER 6
76TH AND STATE

Early that summer, we moved to a brown brick six-flat on 76th and State in the State Street corridor flanking the Englewood and Park Manor neighborhoods. This neighborhood was also black but seemed sleepy, quiet and upscale compared to the ones we had previously lived in. You never heard street noise and I loved that. But the flat was tiny, little more than a studio, and Mother had to sleep on the living room couch. She bought me some roller skates, the clunky all-metal kind you screwed onto your shoes with a key, and I tried to skate down the smooth sidewalks. The skates never stayed on and I never learned to skate but there were no rats-—at all! I'd slip and slide down those sidewalks-—always half-wet from lawn sprinklers and on hot days I breathed in the steamy green odor of drowned grass. There were two little brothers, about my age, living with their mother in the building—-Emmitt and Greg. In the afternoons, we drank Hawaiian Punch and sat on the battleship-gray painted back porch, with the heavy leaves of the trees in the backyard hanging over us like an awning. We shouted the *Witch Doctor Song* chorus over and over—"Oo-ee-oo-ah-ah-ting tang walla-walla-bing bang-oo-ee, oo-ah ah-ting tang walla-walla-bing bang!" until my frazzled mother, off for the summer, dragged me from the steps because we were driving her crazy. The building was pristine and well-maintained and stood on a spotless and well-maintained street, but the City of Chicago almost immediately demolished both to make way for the Dan Ryan Expressway.

The construction of the Dan Ryan expressway destroyed that neighborhood. One day when we were out with my father and his brother Tad, Tad said, shaking his head, "Well, old Master Daley must be happy. That cat's managed to put a permanent wall between his neighborhood (Bridgeport) and all these colored folks he can't stand." So when that summer ended, we lugged our unpacked boxes to our next home in Parkway Gardens.

CHAPTER 7
PARKWAY GARDENS

In the fall of 1958, my brothers, Mother and I, and later my grandparents, moved into the Parkway Gardens public housing project located in the South Side Chicago neighborhood of West Woodlawn. I was nine. The project buildings were sandwiched between the el tracks on 63rd and a scruffy '40's motel on 66th on South Parkway. Parkway Gardens had been built in the late '40's---block after block of stunted sand castles broken occasionally by windows the size and shape of cereal boxes. Across from the Gardens was an assortment of shabby businesses: Scotty's Cleaners whose grungy window sported the shaggy silhouette of a scotty dog and a slogan—"If your clothes are spotty, bring them to Scotty"; a nameless, never-visited, shuttered, veterinarian clinic; and a bustling mom-and-pop convenience store mainly catering to school children with pop, penny candy and "hot bags"—bags of broken potato chips smothered in Louisiana hot sauce. Hanging over the neighborhood like an aromatic mushroom cloud was the charcoal and hickory smoke from Collins' Barbecue House.

Parkway's reputation wasn't as bad as some of the other projects such as the Ida B. Welles and Ickes Homes. From the outside, Parkway looked relatively tidy with well-tended lawns and no broken windows. When we first moved there, there were mice and roaches but they weren't outrageous and there were regular exterminations. There were even apartments in the project that people were said to be buying.

We considered ourselves lucky. We lived in a two- bedroom flat on the first floor of a three-story, walk-up building. These low-rise units were considered to be superior to those in the eight-story buildings, where hoodlums threw garbage in the hallways, disabled elevators, and broke into apartments. My grandparents had left Michigan and come to stay with us permanently as my grandfather's health was worsening. He had started seeing double and having unstoppable episodes of hiccups and nosebleeds. He walked around in his pajamas all day, too exhausted to even dress. My grandparents slept in one of the bedrooms; my mother, my two brothers and I slept in the other. I slept with my mother and the boys in a bunk bed.

On days when Grandpa felt better, he and my grandmother would walk arm and arm to the corner of 63rd and South Parkway to see the old grounds of White City, the famous but long demolished amusement park located at the northern tip of the Parkway Gardens complex. That year it was an almost vacant lot--there was a lone shanty standing in its middle that sold Italian beef, hotdogs and greasy fries. In the summer, one of Chicago's fly-by-night vacant lot neighborhood carnivals camped there and we rode on the rickety Ferris wheel and creaky cramped rides. In the early 60's, an elementary school was built on the lot.

But in those late 1950's days, after walking to the lot, Grandpa'd get what I thought of as his middle-distance, memory face. He'd tell me and Mother the real reason Chicago officials called the park "White City" was because, when he was growing up, "Colored couldn't get in. You could work there but they'd beat you up if you tried to get on the rides or eat a hotdog." My grandparents never elaborated on the White City racial incidents and since they happened long before I was born, I never thought of them or related them to my world. My universe on Chicago's southeast side was and had been totally black. I can't remember ever seeing a white person in any of the neighborhoods we lived in, not even an insurance salesman or a lost motorist and didn't think anything of this. I didn't understand or even know that the rigidity of racial and residential boundaries and the harshness of restrictions on black people's individual and group mobility and freedom were due to still existing prejudice and racism.

CHAPTER 8
ST. MATTHEW'S

We settled in at Parkway and I started at the new school. St. Matthew's was a non-Catholic parochial school, a forlorn, dark brick, el-shaped two-story structure in a leafy, still middle-class black neighborhood on the southeast side. The school was attached to a church that clearly had been magnificent in its heyday (when whites attended it) but now had broken stained glass, cracked plaster, and dry-rotted wood. The church and school belonged to a Protestant denomination that had only recently decided to allow Negroes to join. The denomination may have officially dropped the bar against Negro membership but there was no acknowledgment, support, money or otherwise, as far as I knew, for St. Matthew's church or its school, the sole "colored" grammar school.

The school looked and was run like an underfunded orphanage—dingy, bare walls, concrete or squeaking unfinished wood floors, mismatched, donated carved-up school furniture, with *Lava* soap and sandpapery towels and tissue in the bathroom. The school was never up to code and the principal and school founder, Miss Plymouth, was always asking church members to paint, wire, or jerry-rig the plumbing and electricity in the old school and church in an attempt to satisfy state inspectors.

From my very first day at the school, I could tell learning was going to be secondary. There were about a hundred students in the whole place. The school attracted children whose parents were professionals with decent incomes (doctors, lawyers, teachers, nurses) but who, because of their race or lack of academic achievement, were unwelcome in authentic, elite private schools. There were some kids whose behavior was so incorrigible it even exceeded the tolerance of the public or Catholic school systems for problem students. Then, there were those who had physical or mental developmental disabilities. Today they would be considered special needs children. Their frantic parents shopped around for a school that would take and keep them even if they had to pay. Then there were some like me, who could perform academically and whose parents felt they were too good for the public schools but lacked the money to send them anywhere better. These parents, like my mother, lied to themselves that since it wasn't a public school, it, therefore, had to be a good, even a great, school.

Neither the state certification board nor the denomination's educational hierarchy seemed to question or care about the quality or quantity of the education we were receiving. There was one thing better about St. Matt's though-—no one threatened to beat my butt after school.

St. Matt's didn't hold formal, regular classes that taught history, geography, spelling, or arithmetic. At the beginning of each semester, books(usually used and penciled up by former owners) were passed out only to sit unopened at the edge of our desks. Every morning I'd stand with the other third graders and we'd recite the Ten Commandments, our denomination's catechism, Bible passages or sing hymns like *A Mighty Fortress is Our God* or *Go Down Moses*. At about ten in the morning, we'd go to recess in the school's tiny playground and play tetherball, double-dutch or tag until time for lunch. The most important part of the day was the afternoon--devoted entirely to rehearsing for operetta and concert performances and inter-school competitions. The seventh and eighth graders spent their afternoons practicing for concerts, and choral competitions (the only exception to this Negro school's exclusion from intra-denominational activities) against the white schools in our denomination. There were only about five eighth graders, all girls. They stood most afternoons before the church's altar, led by buttermilk-colored, auburn ringletted Portia Maxwell whose thin soprano led the others in singing "*O Holy Night* and "*I Know a Green Cathedral.*"

The kindergarten through sixth grade students practiced in the basement for the endless series of fairy tale–based "operettas" beloved by Miss Plymouth. She'd remind us daily that these plays were an important source of funds for the school, and during the school year at least one was always in production. The operetta stories were simple and typically revolved around fairy princesses who kissed and transformed frogs who were really princes and menaced by witches and evil kings. The songs had lyrics such as "A little frog in the pond am I" and "Water lilies, water lilies, floating on the pond." Miss Plymouth, a coffee-colored, iron jawed and spined woman, insisted on daily, grueling practice although the final productions remained awkward and amateurish.

Miss Plymouth filled the princess and prince roles with the lightest skinned little girls and boys who had the longest and straightest hair. Even though, at nine, I was the same age as the royal fleet, I acknowledged for the first time what I had long suspected seeing the closeness between my paternal grandmother and my cousins. It was not talent, intelligence, or even good looks, but certain types of looks—butter-pecan skin and silky brown hair--that got the roles. The principal paid little or no attention to me at first but later decided that despite my average brown skin, long enough but overly textured hair, and mature voice, I could fill roles as moderator, mistress of ceremonies, announcer, or chief usher for the operettas or concerts.

The Chit'lin Coast

I was quite bored with the roles Miss Plymouth handed me. They had no color, no flash. My lines were virtually always the same: "Welcome to our school/operetta/play/concert. We hope you'll enjoy, blah, blah..." None of the other children wanted to play these announcer roles. There wasn't even a costume: I was told to wear a navy blue skirt and white blouse. I'd sit there at the side of the stage and wriggle with impatience watching the same scenes played out day after day. I'd think: *I could play a princess and by now I'd know those lines.*

One day, to break the tedium of watching the lily pads (kindergartners) practice their dance while waiting for my turn to announce a scene change, I pulled out a book-- Betty Smith's, *A Tree Grows in Brooklyn*. I'd been enjoying it on the long bus rides to the school. I was so engrossed I didn't hear Miss Plymouth approach and stand over me. My eyes crept up past her run-over, flat-heeled shoes and her plain brown shift to her burnt almond eyes and pursed lips. Glaring at me over her shoulder was Miss Fanning, her unofficial bodyguard, and assistant butt and leg-whipper. Fanning, the sole Caucasian employee (no one knew what she really did) was a razor-lipped scarecrow in gray—-gray face, gray baggy tweeds, gray Dutch boy bob, gray dentures. Gleeful that there was a white person we could safely laugh at, if only behind her back, we kids called Fanning a "bum", because she lived somewhere on the church premises rather than in a home of her own. We enjoyed speculating that the Plymouth family forced her to sleep on the back pews in the church and that's why she never changed her clothes. We conjectured endlessly on how she had ended up living and working with or for black folks. One upper-class girl said she heard Miss Fanning was run out of her white neighborhood for having a colored boyfriend. The thought of any man, black or white, kissing or going further with Miss Fanning made us laugh even harder.

This day though, Miss Plymouth shouted in my face: "Give me that book. It's not about Jesus and it's for grown-ups. If you don't give me that book right now, I'm going to whip your legs." She or Miss Fanning were always whipping girl's legs or threatening to do so.

I quickly relinquished the book, stumbling over an explanation—-"Miss Plymouth, I was going to put it back in my desk." But looking into her angry eyes, I saw a new gleam, a light bulb clicking on. The next morning, she greeted me with one of her fleeting smiles, and informed me crisply that I would no longer have to recite the Commandments or the catechism every morning. She'd heard I was an excellent reader and that meant I could assist her by helping kids who couldn't read well. Miss Plymouth claimed to be proud of me and said she was certain that I'd be a teacher someday. I knew she wasn't really asking me to help her, she was ordering me. I didn't want to do it. At all. But I was too young to know I could have refused or that it was inappropriate and illegal for her to ask. I wanted her attention as a deserving teacher's pet, not as someone forced to listen to other kids stumble over their reading.

So I sat with the third and fourth graders each morning and listened to them bungle Dick and Jane's dull adventures ("Oh-oh, see Sss-Spot, rrr- run.")This became so numbing, day after day, I had trouble staying awake. The fourth through sixth graders were especially a problem. They resented me, a nine-year old, correcting them. Some of them had been promoted along, despite their low achieving performances, but they were still thirteen or fourteen years old and in the fourth or fifth grades. Two of the worst readers were twitchy fraternal teenaged twins, a girl and a boy, fat, scowling, pug-nosed. They both had blotchy liver-yellow skin, and hair as fine and straight as silk thread. Reading sessions with them were especially disastrous as their reading ability seemed to worsen with every session. One horrible session after another culminated with the sister twin shouting at me: "My mother says that I don't have to do what you say because you're only eight! Everyone hates you because you think you're smart!"

My reply, although I was their "teacher" and actually nine, was that of an eight-year old—"I hate y'all, too, and so does my mother!"

In the afternoons, I'd break briefly from listening to the mumblings of the fifth and sixth grade readers and dash through my "Welcome to our operetta and our school" lines in whatever current announcer/greeter role I had been assigned. The whole teaching/listening routine was a waste of time for me and my "pupils". Neither the students nor Plymouth were interested in my efforts or their progress. My eyes glazed over when listening to the reading, and I had no idea how to motivate them. I tried going up to my regular classroom and bragging loudly, "I'm teaching those big kids how to read!" After all, I was the one helping Miss Plymouth. I thought the kids I liked and who I wanted to like me----Ida, Anita, Sandra, Isaac--would be impressed and look up to me. Instead, they'd titter and run out to play rope or catch and I'd sag. No one noticed I was no longer attending classes or expressed envy or interest in what I was doing. Once I assumed the teacher role, neither I nor anyone else thought I was supposed to play with the other children any longer.

For the next year or so, the adults in my life, including my mother, ignored this unorthodox situation, the unfairness to me *and* the poor readers as well as my discomfort with what was going on. I mostly ignored the uncomfortable feeling that this wasn't what the kid's parents or my mother were paying for, because I didn't know what to do about it. My mother seemed flattered that my brain had placed me in a position to "teach" others and bragged to her sisters about it. She preferred to believe that my new role was that of a deserving teacher's pet rather than an unpaid, underage flunky. I think she was just happy that I didn't mention any more schoolyard violence or rat incidents and it didn't occur to me to go into detail about my situation. I wasn't aware of just how much learning I was missing because I had nothing to compare it to, but I suspected things weren't right.

Meanwhile, Miss Plymouth devoted her mornings and afternoons to her musical play and concert sing-off rehearsals. She hired four more teachers to form her staff. There were always rumors that these teachers were at the school because they couldn't pass state licensing or certification exams or they'd done something that made them unemployable in the public school system. While we never knew if that was true, we knew that they acted more like junior prison guards than teachers. One teacher even swore at us and engaged in a cursing match with a third grade girl! Another beat two girls' knuckles with a wood ruler until she broke their fingers and they had to be rushed to the hospital. These teachers lounged around in an empty classroom with their already small loads further lightened by me, smoking or eating potato chips, whipping kids' legs and hands for real and imaginary disciplinary infractions, or jumping to please Miss Plymouth every time she opened her mouth.

After a year and a half, I became increasingly fidgety and started shirking my listening duties. My growing annoyance with grumbling non-readers had reached saturation point. I was afraid of Miss Plymouth but, in desperation, I cornered her during one of the few times she was in her office. She was sitting at her desk, looking idly at some papers. Ignoring Miss Fanning's mean squint, I tattled on the reluctant and defiant "readers". "Miss Plymouth," I blurted, "those kids won't listen to me and their reading is still bad no matter what I do. I told them if they didn't do what I told them, you'd be mad." She didn't even look up at me but said, "Uh, huh. Well, we'll see what happens."

I knew then my usefulness to her was at an end. Besides, I had noticed by then that when graduation time rolled around, Miss Plymouth slapped a hat and gown on all the older non-readers and acted as if she were sending real scholars into the world. After that meeting, I immediately stopped sitting down with the slow readers and just sat in the back of the empty classroom with a book of my own (I alternated my time between Charles Dickens and the *Betsey-Tacy-Tib* series by Maud Hart Lovelace). The readers talked, joked or goofed around. I didn't care. I started going back out to recess. Miss Plymouth ignored me completely and I was glad. Then one day, I got my payoff. Out of the blue, she announced, "Kim, I'm giving you a double promotion from the fourth grade to the sixth grade and you don't have to listen to the reading anymore." She didn't stop to discuss it with me, what it meant, or what had brought it on. I didn't care. I jumped up and down like a demented cheerleader after she walked away because I realized that I could escape the school in a very few years if I played along. Perhaps I would get to a high school where maybe I could learn something new.

Shortly after abruptly relieving me of my duties, Miss Plymouth disappeared down south somewhere for year or so, reportedly on family business. I felt as if I'd been released from jail. She left her brother in charge as acting principal.

CHAPTER 9
ST. MATT'S AGAIN

Brother Cedric Plymouth was smarter, kinder, and better-looking than his sister. He had drowsy, camel-lashed eyes with a wide, white, movie villain's smile. He'd previously taught at a public school and was slightly more focused on teaching than his sister. He'd conduct civics classes in which we would discuss how poorly Negroes were treated in the South and what Dr. King should do next to help us all gain our rights. The unrelenting fixation on musicals and singing was also eliminated. "Mother", I said, "Guess what? We won't have to be in any more operettas 'cause Brother Plymouth doesn't want to do them." Mother jumped up and did an impromptu jig, "Thank God! I am so sick of giving up my Sundays to go and hear all that bad singing in those horrible kiddy musicals. I hope that old Miss Plymouth never comes back."

Although I didn't say anything about it to my mother, however, I thought I noticed Brother Plymouth let his hands drift occasionally across the budding breasts and butts of my female classmates. He'd also announce frequently to the class, smiling widely, "That Kim is so smart—--just look at her. She can listen to what I'm saying and read a book at the same time. Now that's brains." Although still shy, I liked his praise but carefully avoided being alone with him and his wandering hands.

Brother also couldn't seem to fill the days up with schoolwork. Most afternoons, I could hear the older girls and boys bopping and twisting in the abandoned '40's bowling alley in the school basement to the wail of *Any Day Now* by Chuck Jackson or the thump, thump, thump of the *Duke of Earl* by Gene Chandler.

Although I didn't have to deal with the readers any longer, I was restless during the day because we still didn't have regular classes. Neither Brother Plymouth nor the other children seemed to miss me when I slipped out of class or didn't return from recess. I had started hanging around the cafeteria and helping the cook.

I loved being around food and food preparation. The head cook was a very fat woman with smooth caramel skin and washboard hair waves named Mrs. Fulton. She waddled around alone in the kitchen, breathing heavily, after the other cook was fired for being caught without a hair net by the food inspectors. I think Mrs. Fulton was lonely. My help in the kitchen didn't amount to much but she seemed to appreciate it. The calm rhythm of the large, old-fashioned kitchen and good but unimaginative cooking gave me a peaceful feeling. Mrs. Fulton cooked Mississippi favorites such as tomato pudding made with buttered bread, tomatoes and sugar, baked macaroni and cheese, smothered chicken, cornmeal-fried perch, meatloaf and mashed potatoes swimming in salty brown gravy and devil's food cake with chocolate butter cream frosting. I cut up tomatoes, sprinkled cheese on macaroni, ladled melted butter on Wonder bread triangles, dribbled gravy in mashed potato valleys, wrapped up silverware in napkins, and placed them on the trays. I washed dishes and sold potato chips, Twinkies and Hostess cupcakes to the kids.

I got a free lunch in return and avoided Mother's brown-bag lunches of limp summer sausage sandwiches and peanut butter with no jelly. Best of all, I could pitch her weekly Kraft pimiento or pineapple cheese sandwiches which I really hated. At that time, my grandparents were still living with us because of Grandpa's increasing debilitation. Unfortunately, despite my grandmother's considerable energy and superior cooking skills, she didn't take over the cooking from my mother. After day after day of cheap, humdrum meals like tuna casserole and tough lamb stew, I couldn't take it anymore. "Mother, when are we going to have something good? I hate this stuff." Mother got a suffering look on her face. "If you don't like it you can go without! I go out in the cold and snow to that old school to feed y'all and this is what you got to say to me? You all are so ungrateful!" My grandmother chimed in, snapping, "Stop complaining and try to be a help to your mother!"

The winter I was eleven, my grandparents returned to Michigan, and shortly thereafter Grandpa died. His heart and kidneys had finally given out. Although we kids had spent a lot of time with Grandpa, had witnessed and worried about his slow and painful decline, and wanted to say goodbye to him, Mother refused to let us attend the funeral. She, my aunts and uncle went to Idlewild to bury him alone. When Mother returned, she told us, with no elaboration "Grandma's staying up in Idlewild for now." Grandpa was rarely ever mentioned again.

Meanwhile, I went to that school for two more years but skipped classes and learned virtually nothing. It was as if I was an almost invisible employee. When I wasn't helping Mrs. Fulton, Brother Plymouth asked me to carry messages and mail around the school and to help in the office, which irritated Mrs. Maxwell, the school secretary who didn't like me.

Both my cafeteria and messenger duties came to a sudden halt, however, when I surprised Brother Plymouth and Mrs. Maxwell in what appeared to even my naive eyes to be a sexually compromising situation. One day I skipped up to his office with a message and found the door half closed. I pushed it open and walked in and saw Mrs. Maxwell, on her knees, sobbing with her arms thrown around Brother

Plymouth's legs and her face buried in his crotch. He frowned down at her while she gasped and tried to talk between sobs: "I can't bear it if you leave me. I thought we were going to be together." Brother suddenly saw me. He didn't look startled or ashamed although he was supposed to be a man of God and was married as was Mrs. Maxwell.

When she finally noticed me, she covered her eyes and cried even harder. I couldn't think of a thing to say. I was riveted to the floor. I felt as shocked as if I had seen them having sex, but at the same time I had a lightning flash desire to giggle since Mrs. Maxwell had always given me a hard time about late tuition checks and made her contempt for me crystal clear. Brother Plymouth stood up straight, looked me coldly in the eye and thundered, "Go back to the classroom right now! I don't want to see you working in that kitchen any more or carrying messages. "You're supposed to be a student here, not an employee." I was eleven and I had been fired.

CHAPTER 10
GRADUATION

I graduated from St. Matt's when I was twelve. I wasn't sorry to leave St. Matt's, and despite my pride in graduating and moving onward, I left steamed at what I perceived to be unfair treatment. During my last two years at the school, I'd been promised several times by both Miss Plymouth and her brother that I would be the valedictorian of the class. During my last year, in the eighth grade, they admitted a girl, Pamela Olden, who was the daughter of one of the few black baseball players on a major-league Chicago team. Pamela looked like a chubby, cheerful beaver and wore her dry hair skinned back in a thin ponytail. She bragged a lot. "My daddy is rich. He's a big baseball player and buys me everything I want," she reminded us every day. As far as the schoolwork went, she didn't seem dumb or smart, but then hadn't been given anything to prove either way. Only days before graduation, I was called into Miss Plymouth's office. Her tone and message were short: "Pamela Olden's going to be the valedictorian this year. Kim. You'll be the salutatorian." I felt betrayed, hurt and flabbergasted. I veered between faintness and vertigo. Hot tears ran backward and closed my throat. I wanted to throw Miss Plymouth's framed desk picture of Jesus at her ugly face. I stood there feeling shrunken, my body broiling and freezing. I'd never worried about being valedictorian, I just understood I would be--the deserving center of attention and admiration for once on graduation day. Tasting unshed tears and with my voice wobbling, I reminded Miss Plymouth, who had returned from the south that year, "I thought it was decided that I'd be the val." She said dismissively, "You all took a test. She did better on it than you."

I almost staggered with disbelief at what I just heard. I couldn't hold back my tears on the bus ride home. I'd been there for years outperforming the other students with what little we'd been given and, in fact, had done Plymouth's job—teaching—-for a long while. I'd worked in the school's office and kitchen because I had already mastered what little schoolwork they gave me. Pamela had just arrived and spent all her time crowing about her dad's money. She'd never taken any test, as Miss Plymouth claimed, but had spent every afternoon twisting and bopping in the basement to the lovesick moans of the Drifters and Frankie Lymon on scratchy '45s. In fact, there had been no test.

I ran home and told my mother. "Miss Plymouth is going to let Pamela Olden be the valedictorian instead of me. She always said it was going to be me!" I said with more tears dripping down my face. Mother's shoulders drooped and she sighed but said nothing. That Sunday on the way to the movies, I ranted to my father and begged him, "Please call Miss Plymouth or Brother Plymouth and tell them I'm supposed to be the valedictorian."

He reared back against his headrest and yelled—"You're smarter than her. You know stuff she'll never know. They're just letting her be the valedictorian because Butch Olden plays for the Sox!" Despite my pleas, though, neither parent would call the Plymouths and make a fuss about the unfair decision.

The night of the graduation ceremony, wearing the required pouffy white dress with its silky graduation bosom ribbon, I sullenly greeted the gathered parents and friends and rushed, slouching, through my salutatory speech. With my disdainful body language, I was determined to show my scorn for the whole ceremony and Pamela, although as I gazed around I could see that no one in the audience noticed or cared. I dramatically rolled my eyes and sat with arms crossed throughout Pamela's valedictory speech. My surliness exploded, albeit inwardly, when all the girl graduates were ceremoniously handed bouquets of roses by their families. Neither of my parents had thought to do that. The terrible night was capped by the fact that after the ceremony, the other graduates were whisked off by their parents to dinner at restaurants. At the end of the ceremony, Mother came up to me and said, "Let's go home." My father had already left. I thought I'd never recover at the time, but little by little the incident faded.

CHAPTER 11
BACK TO PARKWAY GARDENS WITH A SIDE TRIP TO 63RD STREET

Our Parkway apartment, like its predecessors, backed onto a square of asphalt and gravel, an open area that served as our parking lot and playground. If the concrete balconies were our picket fences, this space was our town square, the hard and treeless surface where the Parkway community lived, laughed, played, and fought. Each apartment's back door opened onto the parking lot. I don't remember ever using the front door. I'd shoot out the back door, past the bad Perry brothers' bad dog Lady, and straight through my friends' back doors or zag left into the playground.

When we'd lived in the Gardens for about two weeks, my youngest brother fell off the top of the slide in the playground but thankfully wasn't seriously hurt. One of the neighbors who'd seen the fall, Brenda Jones, helped scoop up my brother and comfort me and my crying mother. And that's how I met my first best friend. Brenda was a bit older than me, plump, cocoa-skinned, with an overbite and Coke-bottle glasses. She was not pretty or even cute but she was street savvy and knowing about the world in a way I wasn't. I went to St. Matt's and she went to James McCosh, the local public school. After school and on weekends, I'd race out our back door and across the lot to Brenda's. We didn't spend too much time at my house because my mother didn't like Brenda: "That old Brenda's too fast, and she rolls her eyes at me when she thinks I'm not looking. I heard her telling you those dirty jokes—I don't want you hanging around with her." I ignored everything Mother said. I liked Brenda and wanted to be just like her. Sometimes, we'd meet in the playground with our makeshift jump ropes, which were really plastic clotheslines. We'd spend hours soaking the clotheslines because we'd been told by older jumpers that was necessary to stiffen and season them. Then, we turned them furiously for about an hour—it was called beating them--to prepare for the frequent and all-important neighborhood double-dutch competitions. Or, we'd practice baton twirling—-we wanted to be majorettes--at which we were terrible. We ran screaming together from the theater at the end of *Psycho,* enjoyed sobbing during the funeral in *Imitation of Life* and loved shrieking on the Bobs and Fireball rides at the Riverview Amusement Park on Chicago's northwest side.

    I liked going to Brenda's apartment and, as I approached my teens, dancing the Madison (I liked the Jackie Gleason "away we go" steps and the Wilt Chamberlain basketball dunking steps) or bop dancing to the Drifters or Miracles. At times, we'd just sit around on her porch and complain about our schools or we'd talk about other girls we knew: who had the sharpest clothes or the "best" hair.

    Brenda's apartment was one bedroom larger than ours. All day, Brenda's extremely fat mother sat on their dingy orange slip-covered couch, legs spread widely, panties showing. She was always watching tv, usually reruns. Although Brenda claimed her mother worked at a drycleaners, I never saw her leave the house or the couch. She never smiled, chatted or even looked directly at her children but stared,

The Chit'lin Coast

silently and grimly, at Lucy Ricardo's grape-stomping or Ralph Cramden's yelling and scheming.

What I liked best about Brenda was that she surrounded herself with and sang "hip" music unlike the square songs and singers like Rosemary Clooney and Dinah Washington my mother listened to on our Zenith radio. While I sounded like a seagull when I sang, Brenda sang so well she was even in a Shirelles-type girl group at McCosh. She could solo on songs like *Shop Around* by The Miracles and *This Is Dedicated To The One I Love*. I watched and listened with the other kids in the parking lot, my mouth hanging open in wonder, when she sang *Chantilly Lace*, because she could boom "Oh, baby" deep like the Big Bopper, a dude, then turn around and sing sweet and high-pitched like Mary Wells on *The One Who Really Loves You*.

My family didn't own a stereo or even a record player. The only time I got to hear music that was not square was at Brenda's house. We couldn't have afforded records even if we had a player since my mother was a single parent and there was little money for leisure activities or "toys". My father sent his $60 a month, not much even in those days, for child support for three children. Case closed-—he wasn't contributing a cent more.

So I never had had any records to play on Brenda's portable pink and black record player, unlike the others in our neighborhood group. But someone visiting us once left behind an Elvis Presley 45 of *Heartbreak Hotel* which I'd heard him sing on the radio. I dug his throaty and smooth voice. I didn't know then that the song was about three years old, and not really new. I couldn't wait to show Brenda I not only owned a record-—-but an Elvis record.

I pounded up Brenda's stairs clutching the record. But when I proudly showed it to her, she snatched it from me, looked at the label, made a sound of disgust and threw it on the floor. "Girl, we can't listen to this! Don't you know Elvis said that all a nigger can do for him is shine his shoes and buy his records?" I was stunned. I had not heard that. I felt like a shamed child, always the last to know about things that mattered to Negroes. Brenda always knew what was happening with our race and talked authoritatively about it. I had been riveted by her stories of filing past her classmate Emmett Till's beaten body at his wake, watching the murdered Sam Cooke's hearse roll by our building, and even showing me the Jet magazine article and (gulp!) photos of the woman's head found in a wastebasket at a local black hotel.

I vaguely knew Elvis was from the South, supposedly the land where all prejudice resided, but my awareness of the civil rights movement and southern behavior was limited mostly to having watched TV news reports of the Montgomery bus boycott and the integration of Central High in Little Rock. Still, I'd never heard of a nationally recognized celebrity such as Elvis openly voicing such views, although according to Brenda, my parents and other black adults, most whites hated Negroes whether they publicly admitted it or not. I looked down at the Elvis 45 lying on Brenda's rug, miraculously unbroken. I picked it up and left Brenda's house, feet dragging, disgraceful record in hand. The minute I got in the house, I repeated Elvis's words to my mother. She didn't seem scandalized or even interested in the awful Elvis remark: she shrugged one shoulder. "Flower, don't forget it's your turn to wash the dishes tonight." I threw the Elvis 45 high on a bedroom closet shelf and promptly forgot it. I thought the subject of Elvis would be closed forever.

By then, my parents had been divorced a couple of years, and when we got to the age where we'd sit quietly in a theater, my father started taking my brothers and me to the movies every Sunday. That's all we ever did with him. He'd pull up in a parking space behind our back door, often in his postman uniform, and we'd jump in. Sometimes we'd stop by McDonald's, then a new hamburger chain that had opened up in our neighborhood, and pick up their burgers and fries which we liked better than White Castle's.

We didn't talk much on the way which was only about four blocks. "And I said to myself, it's wonderful, wooonderful", Dad would sing (loudly and badly) Nat King Cole or Johnny Mathis tunes like *Wonderful* or would sing along with the radio as if he wanted to avoid talking to us. When the movie ended, he dumped us in the parking lot outside our apartment. There was no chatting--he never asked us about school, hobbies, or what we might be thinking or, in my case, worrying about. He never told us what he had done with his week nor invited us to any events or gatherings other than the Sunday movies. He was happy being a mystery to us.

Sometimes he'd hold me back and question me about whether Mother was seeing men and mutter threats about her having men around us. "Tell her I want to come back!" he'd demand, tears falling suddenly and silently down his face. I hated these talks and became wary of them. I felt embarrassed that he let me see him, an adult man and a father, cry. I also wasn't convinced that his tears were real. They never appeared before we got to our apartment. I started poising myself to jump out of the car the minute he pulled up behind our unit. I never admitted anything about Mother's occasional dates. I'd had enough of their trouble and fighting, when we lived on Hubbard and Ellis, to last me forever and resented being placed in the middle of their ongoing and revenge-based post-divorce battle.

In any event, my father had a fiancée, Sukie, an unfriendly Alabama woman with a nondescript but mean face. Sometimes she'd come to the movies with us, sitting silently between us and Dad with crossed arms, making our uncomfortable outings even more so. She and Dad never touched or even spoke to one another. When I asked him why he decided to marry her, since he didn't seem to be in love with her or she with him, he was blunt: "She makes good money and gives me the check." I couldn't understand why that kind of marriage would satisfy anyone. I was naïve and believed most marriages were based on love, at least initially, although I knew my parents' was not. I also wondered why he claimed to care if Mother saw someone too. It wasn't as if he and Mother had had a good marriage or that reconciliation was even a possibility. When I told Mother about his questions and the new girlfriend, she said, "That shrimp! He can ask all he wants. I'm never going back to him. He can go on and marry that woman. I don't care."

Going to the movies with Dad meant ending up at one of three nearby Woodlawn neighborhood theaters---we never ventured south or north of 63rd Street, the main drag in Woodlawn. Each sat in the shadow of the el structure that ran down "our" part of 63rd Street sweeping eastward from South Parkway to Stony Island. The fanciest and most expensive was a genuine art deco movie palace--the Tivoli--where you could see first-run movies featuring stars like Paul Newman and Elizabeth Taylor. We didn't get there much. The Maryland was an average neighborhood theater featuring B and sometimes A movies with actors like Troy Donahue and Sandra Dee, the golden twins of soapy teen movies and pastel romances. The Ark was a dump. Its marquee lights were all busted out and the names of the movies had missing letters. The Ark movies featured Z list actors in grade C crime, cowboy and war flicks whose names we never remembered. At the Ark, rats ran over our feet to get at the popcorn and gum under the seats. The heavy air always smelled of sweat, hamburgers, popcorn, and something nasty but unidentifiable. Unruly teenage boys walked around during the movies fighting and throwing food at one another. The ushers, also teenage boys, either ran up and down the aisles stopping fights or stood woodenly watching the movies and ignoring the chaos. There was so much noise at the Ark everything was drowned out except the endless movie gunfire. Since my father always claimed to be, as he put it, "broker than the Ten Commandments", and because money dictated all his viewing decisions, we naturally spent most of our time at the Maryland or the Ark seeing whatever was playing.

One Sunday when I was about fourteen, Dad announced that it was a Maryland Sunday and the Maryland's featured movie was *Blue Hawaii*, starring Elvis Presley. The movie was about two years old by then but in those days, the Maryland never got new releases. Actually,

The Chit'lin Coast

I yearned to see Elvis and still secretly liked his voice but was nervous about whether this was a racially okay thing for a black person to do. But if I acted unenthusiastic about the Maryland, we might end up at that funky Ark. So, even though I hadn't mentioned Elvis to anyone or even thought much about him since the incident at Brenda's, I asked my father, "Daddy, did you hear that Elvis said all Negroes could do for him was shine his shoes and buy his records?"

"I don't care what that cracker said." Dad scoffed as he pulled up in front of the Maryland. "He don't run my life and I'm never gonna shine his damn shoes or buy his records. All I got is Maryland money this week. It's either that or nowhere."

Fan-tas-tic! I danced on air into the Maryland behind Dad and the boys. As usual, we had stuffed our secret stash of McDonald's hamburgers and Big Time candy bars under our coats since Dad refused to buy the overpriced candy and chewy-stale popcorn sitting in the fly-specked glass cases at the Maryland.

I kept my fingers crossed that no black person I knew would see me going to an Elvis movie or, for that matter, going to the movies with my father and little brothers. Once safely in my moldy smelling seat in the dark, I sank down, feet stuck to the sticky floor, and leaned back in bliss. Ah! Palm trees, white sand, Hawaiian beaches! Hips swiveling, sports car-driving, fists flying, Elvis beat up the other guys in the movie over some chicks in beehive hairdos. Best of all, Elvis's voice poured romance over us like melted butter on movie popcorn. I floated out of the theater. I no longer had to worry about Brenda's disapproval—we'd left Parkway and moved to East Woodlawn that year and our friendship had ended even before the move. I did mention seeing and liking it to one of my black high school classmates. She looked at me with lofty scorn. "Kim, that fool said that all we could do for him was shine his shoes and buy his records. You ought to be ashamed to admit you went and saw him."

Sixty-third street was our Main Street, our LaSalle Street, our State Street, our Magnificent Mile. Our stretch of 63rd street ran from

South Parkway all the way to Stony Island, and in our imagination crossed Jackson Park and ended in the Lake. During the work week, the Woodlawn community could conduct all its business there. There were square-built, serious looking banks with tellers wearing green eyeshades, "dirty window" doctor and lawyer offices, beauty parlors, wig and record stores, dry goods and hardware stores, clinics and a welfare office. There were movie theaters, bars and lounges, and soul food restaurants like Daly's, with its mouth-watering smothered chicken livers and onions. There was the fish market whose owner refused to scale or gut fish for my mother no matter how much she begged or argued. There was the Hi-Low grocery store where we fished boxes of Kraft macaroni and cheese and Swanson pot pies out of a barrel for ten cents apiece. The big cross streets of South Parkway and Cottage Grove were each capped by a gleaming white-tiled Walgreen's drug store, whose windows contained two big apothecary jars filled with green and red liquid. Both Walgreens featured soda fountain and counter service. I can't remember getting anything from the pharmacy but I always bee-lined to the lunch counter. In those days, Walgreens served fries the way I liked them: limp and fatty, with dark chocolatey real malts, not those imposters--milk shakes. The malts were thick with ice cream and real whipped cream. As far as I was concerned, the other star of the counter was the grilled cheese sandwich, each bite a wonder of oozed butter and gooey American cheese.

Because of its iron canopy, the el train tracks, 63rd street was perpetually dark, which actually added to its festive, almost night-clubby air. The only light at night, beside the neon of the taprooms and the nightclubs were those smoky little platform lights peeking through the el structure and rails. The el roared through all day and much of the night but everyone was used to it and not disturbed. In fact, the deafening rumble made it seem as if important stuff was happening—-people were traveling here or leaving here to go downtown. People strolled the streets, shopping, talking, laughing, arguing at all times of the day and night, seeing and being seen. The sweet falsetto sounds of the Platters or the Supremes streamed from every storefront, while barbecue smoke and the greasy popcorn smell of burned hair from the beauty parlors hazed the air. I'd see drag queens in full evening dress and makeup even during the day, brothers whose hair was styled in slick and orangey chemical processes or "conks" as we called them (modeled after the actor Paul Newman's in the movie *Quo Vadis*), prostitutes, mothers, fathers, schoolchildren, old people. I tagged happily behind my mother on her weekly and sometimes daily errands on 63rd with an extra wave at my favorite sight: a gentleman, probably in his seventies, who stood smiling in front of the Walgreen's at Cottage Grove. He was always dressed in perfect, 1920's style: straw hat skimmer, creased baggy pants, suspenders, high collared shirt cinched with a jaunty bow tie, ice cream jacket, and best of all spats---white apron inserts---on his shoes. Saturday nights, the street hummed with a jubilant, party air.

No one in our family knew how to swim at that time, but we made short trips east on 63rd street to the Jackson Park beach. Since we lived so close, Mother felt we should try to appreciate being near the lake even if we did nothing but wade. We never enjoyed ourselves or stayed long. The beach was always littered, rocky, the sand dirty and clinging, and there was nothing to buy or eat that I can remember so we had to bring our own fried chicken.

I would hear from others, familiar with the North
Side, that the North Avenue Beach was the place to go: there were sunners and swimmers, refreshment stands, lifeguards, and it was near the marinas where you could see the boats. Every summer though, I'd read articles in the Tribune describing the racial disturbances that occurred whenever Negroes tried to visit that beach, so I didn't expect to ever go there.

We didn't just travel east on 63rd, sometimes we'd travel west to Halsted in Englewood, where we'd buy dollar shoes at the old Southtown movie theater which had been converted to a discount shoe palace. I'd buy loafers for a dollar and stick a penny in the toe slot and pay another dollar for a pair of white gym shoes. The loafers barely lasted through two rains as the soles wore out almost instantly, but they looked good on the first day of school. I'd cut out replacement inner soles from cardboard grocery cartons and use them until the shoes melted off my feet. The gym shoes would last a little longer if I didn't wash them.

CHAPTER 12

PARKWAY COOKING LESSONS

I had always been interested in food and cooking and had gladly assisted the cook at St. Matt's. By the time I was eleven, my mother had started relying on me to start dinner which mainly involved thawing a block of Birdseye frozen green beans or spinach, opening a package of Kraft macaroni and cheese or making hamburger patties to go with a supermarket iceberg lettuce and cardboard flavored tomato salad. I didn't need any imagination or skill to cook those things and they were uninspired in taste and execution. I had started baking simple yellow or chocolate sheet cakes but I still felt unsatisfied with my efforts. My mother couldn't see why a young girl would even be interested in cooking beyond the basics. My relationship with my best friend at the time, Brenda Jones, didn't end well, but to some degree I owe her for giving my interest in cooking some inspiration and direction before we fell out forever.

This is how it began: "Hi girl!" whispered Brenda Jones to me one summer morning in 1959, as she kicked open the screen door and held it open with her foot. "Be quiet!" she stage-whispered. "My Daddy's 'sleep." She let me step past her into their box of a kitchen.

As I passed through it, I noticed a number of still steaming pots covered by chipped dishes on the stove. I was always curious about food in other people's apartments, and I asked Brenda what was in the pots. Brenda glanced indifferently towards the stove, "Oh that's just some grits Mama cooked this morning for breakfast. I didn't want none. I'm gonna go get a plumagranate for breakfast at the Del Farm. Wanna come with me?" "Plumagranate" was Brenda's word for pomegranate. I had tried to be enthusiastic about the lumpy, faded red fruits but trying to dig the tiny, individual seeds out of their bitter membrane and eat them was maddening to me. The infinitesimal burst of sour juice you got from eating the small seeds was not worth it. Brenda loved them, though, and eating them was a deeply enjoyable summer experience for her. I stopped cold. "What are grits?"

Brenda stopped and thought. "Something like porridge or mush."

"Will your mother get mad if I look?" I asked. I was already lifting the cracked china plate and looking down at a white creamy cereal that looked something like Cream of Wheat——not one of my favorites. But there was a miniature butter sun in the middle of the grits and specks of pepper dotted throughout.

Brenda sighed impatiently and said, "You look like you want some. Mama won't care." I silently agreed. I doubted her mother would notice.

My mother objected to my eating at other's homes, usually on vague sanitation grounds, and disapproved of the fact that Mrs. Jones did not make her large family sit down and eat together for regular meals but just left the food on the range to be eaten on the run. Mother wasn't around though and I couldn't resist. I pulled a chair out and sat down. I loved tasting unfamiliar foods. I spooned a flowing river of grits onto a plate along with some cold scrambled eggs Brenda apathetically pointed to. Oh my God! It was love at first bite. The corny and buttery goodness of the velvety but slightly grainy cereal slid over my tongue and down my throat. Why had I never had or even been told about this cereal? This beat oatmeal and everything

The Chit'lin Coast

else I ever ate for breakfast. I swirled the scrambled eggs around in the center so they could soak up some of the golden pond. That made it all taste that much better.

While I ate, Brenda was getting dressed and rushed back in the kitchen. "Are you ready to go outside? Brenda ducked back into the living room and whined loudly, "Mama I want some money to get me a plumagranate! Hey, Flower's eating the grits up. She says she never heard of them," Brenda added.

"Brenda Jean, I just gave you some money for candy yesterday," her mother grumbled. She didn't look at Brenda but at Lucy and Ethel, hands on hips, sassing Fred and Ricky. Brenda broke into her "gimme some money" ritual: full throated sobs, accusations of parental neglect and hatred. I heard the familiar sound of Brenda's mother's purse opening and change clinking. "And don't come back asking for no more money!" she shouted.

I was still not through with those grits, though. I got up and spooned more onto my plate and shook salt and pepper over it quickly. Brenda came back in the kitchen with several dollars clutched in her hand, tears drying already. When she saw I was still eating, she said "Wanna hear a joke?" Brenda possessed a seemingly endless stockpile of dirty and racially offensive jokes.

"I guess so," I said as I dragged a piece of crispy bacon I had seen under another plate on the stove through the second helping.

"Ooh", said Brenda, "Well, a white man went into a meat store to get some meat for his cat..." All of Brenda's many jokes and rhymes seemed to involve a white man who became frustrated with the joke's fact situations, followed by a Chinese man(that's the only Asian group anyone in our community seemed to know about) who was similarly frustrated. The colored man (as we called them in those days) then stepped in, super-brainy, spouted the dirty punch line, and solved the problem.

I rolled my last bit of bacon in the last bit of grits and tuned out Brenda's story until I realized she had reached the colored man part of the joke. "And the colored man said, put your motherfucking money on the motherfucking floor and get your motherfucking ass out the motherfucking door!" Brenda crowed triumphantly, not even lowering her voice so her mother couldn't hear the curse words. I laughed, slapped my hand over my mouth and cast a quick eye at Brenda's mother's back. I could hear Lucy wailing in her baby cry as she begged Ricky to let her do something. Brenda's mother said nothing. Maybe Brenda's mother (and, God forbid, her sleeping father) didn't hear that joke.

We left and as we walked to Del Farms through the smog of barbecue smoke from a nearby "Q" joint, I asked Brenda how her mother fixed the grits. "Oh, I don't know. She just throws them in the water and boils them I think," Brenda said without interest. Later that day, I asked my mother if we could have grits for breakfast from then on as I had eaten them at Brenda's and thought they were delicious. "Flower, I thought I told you not to eat at other people's houses. You don't know what diseases they might have or how clean they are." I was always surprised at my mother's objections to my eating other people's food. She was a slapdash cook, always rushed, and not inventive or really curious about new foods. There were some things she made well—fried chicken, steaks, potato salad and spaghetti, but for the most part her cooking was flat, underseasoned and too dependent on frozen or canned foods.

"I'm from the North", Mother haughtily continued. "I don't know anything about southern foods and the types of things these people from Mississippi and Alabama eat."

I persisted, "Do you think there's a recipe in your Better Homes and Gardens cookbook?"

"No, I don't," Mother said. "They don't have things in there like that. You have to be southern to know how to fix stuff like that." It was important to Mother to remind me that although we were black, we didn't have to eat what other black people did. That ended the subject for a time.

I didn't care if a particular food was southern, too black, too poor-folksy or not if I liked it. Besides, most of the other black kids I knew had come from the South, some recently, or were the children of southerners. They all had southern relatives they visited regularly. In fact, southern food and culture had become the base culture of the black neighborhoods of the southeast side as far as I could see. That was my world and I didn't see anything wrong with it.

The next time Mother and I went grocery shopping at the A&P, I ran over to the hot cereal aisle and grabbed a box of Quaker grits. When I presented it to Mother, who had a set, unvarying grocery list, who never bought on impulse, and whose check for two weeks of groceries for four or even six people was always exactly $25.00, she resisted. I was no Brenda and I abhorred girly crying tantrums, but I stamped my foot angrily. Surprised at my unusually resolute behavior, she relented. I was overjoyed and saw that the cooking directions were on the box. From then on several times a week, I prepared grits along with eggs, bacon or sausage. Mother never would eat or fix them, and ignored my brothers and me while we were eating them. But even today, grits are on the list of my ten favorite things to eat.

Grits were not my only food discovery while I was friends with Brenda Jones. One evening in 1959 during the Christmas holiday season, I went over to her apartment to see what she thought she was going to get for Christmas. She always had a long list of wants and she liked talking about them, and, I didn't mind listening. Her excitement was contagious. My brothers and I didn't do too well at Christmas. My mother always told us that as a single parent she just didn't have the money to get us much. My father would go down to Maxwell Street and buy a big bag of assorted boys' and girls' sox or panties/briefs in discontinued or flawed grab-bag sizes and present them to us as a sort of group Christmas gift. They never fit or were too stained or torn to wear. We'd long given up compiling lists since we never got what we asked for.

Brenda had two parents both working **and** living together and, even with four siblings, had seemed to get everything she wanted the previous Christmas—-the Cootie game, '45 records, a transistor radio, new dresses, a pink Princess phone. When Brenda didn't get what she wanted, she could and would cry and pout for days.

As I entered her kitchen, I noticed there was a giant pot on the stove covered by an even bigger chipped platter. And the kitchen smelled funny, funky but there was an elusive and unfamiliar but tempting odor layered under the funk. It smelled like...... I couldn't say what. When I asked her what it was, Brenda lifted the lid and said, "Chit'lins." What looked to me like dirty rags, she explained were chit'lins, or hog bowels. It seems her mama had cleaned and picked twenty pounds of them that day, then had thrown white vinegar, an onion and a white potato in the water with a bay leaf to cut the famously obnoxious odor. According to Brenda, the 20 pounds had boiled down to ten by the time I looked under the lid.

Although Brenda claimed to dislike chit'lins, she was full of informational details. According to her, to ensure that the chit'lins were clean her mother soaked them in Tide detergent after peeling off their top layer of dirty fat. After a thorough scrubbing, they were cooked for thirteen hours so they would be as soft and limp as dishrags. Her mother always served them with spicy "po' folks spaghetti", where the sauce was mixed with the pasta, and celery seed cole slaw. I was not a picky or fearful eater and I asked Brenda if I could have a bite. Brenda insisted, "Have mine. I don't like 'em, especially 'cause I know where they come from on the pig and I seen them pull the guts out of one down in Louisiana. Plus, you can smell 'em all the way down to the parking lot. But Mama makes them every Christmas anyway."

I was well aware of the sights and sounds of pig slaughtering, thanks to the visits to Mother Blake's in Idlewild, but had never heard her or my grandmother mention chit'lins.

Brenda threw some on a plate and liberally doused them with a splash from an always-present bottle of hot sauce. She added a dollop of beefy spaghetti spiced with red pepper and mayonnaisey cole slaw with celery seeds that peeked between the cabbage shreds. While she was dishing this up, she was laughing at me for not knowing what chit'lins were or how they tasted: like earthy, porky ribbons. She couldn't believe I had never heard of them when we had accompanied my grandmother to Mother Blake's. Then she shook her head in amazement because she couldn't see how I could stand them. Brenda swore she had never met anyone in our small, all-black world who didn't know what they were especially in Woodlawn. "People around here either love or hate 'em," she said and that has turned out to be mostly true. I've discovered there were folks who hated the smell but would eat them anyway and those who hated the smell so much they wouldn't eat them and those like myself who were indifferent to the smell because they were so tasty. One thing I learned was that the only people who eat chit'lins in Chicago or anywhere else in America, are, for the most part, African-American (although I now see them on some Chinese restaurant menus). Chit'lins are and have been viewed, by many, as an embarrassing and smelly remnant and reminder of Jim Crow and segregation eating, like hog maws and collards, or as something that only blacks have consumed because white people wouldn't eat them and left them as garbage for blacks. They are and have always been considered to be an outcast food for outcasts.

That day Brenda, as always, got bored watching me eat what her mother had fixed. "I want a big pickle with some Lik-m-ade on it, not this ole stuff", she complained. She had recently developed a passion for sour, dry Lik-m-ade drink powder (it looked and tasted like cheap, fluorescent Kool-Ade) sprinkled on a huge dill pickle or even on her palm. I ignored her and kept gobbling the chit'lins and sides. Delicious! Out of the corner of my eye, I could see Brenda's mother staring at the TV while the actor Robert Stack, as Elliot Ness of the

Untouchables, blasted bad guys and warned mobsters in slow, ghostly tones. Brenda cautioned me:

"My Daddy's gonna want some. You better quit eating them things, Flower. He's gonna be mad if he comes home and they're gone after Mama spent all that time cleaning them."

I finally let her drag me away from the pot, and we made one of our frequent treks for the pickle and powder to the "school" store—the mom and pop store across the street mostly patronized by Parkway school children. In those days, stores like this seemed to be located on every corner on Chicago's South Side. On the way there, Brenda told me a new joke poem. I couldn't stop thinking about the chit'lins though and so only caught the last verse: "The Chinese man said: apples, peaches, pears and plums, me no stop till baby comes." She laughed uproariously and I chuckled even though I really hadn't been listening to the first part. I asked her how her mother made the chit'lins. She said, "I told you. She cleans them, throws them in some Tide or Cheer and then boils them with some onions so they won't stink. The onions and potatoes soak up the odor."

That night I ran home and told my mother about my newest delicious food find and how I wished we could make some at home, Mother said, "Whoa. I have no idea how to make those. I am **not** from the south. Your Uncle (referring to an uncle by marriage from Louisiana) forced my sister to learn how to clean and cook those things. Don't even ask me to learn how to cook them."

Some time later, one of my paternal uncles married Eloise, a South Side girl. She was a pretty good soul cook and agreed to show me how to fix chit'lins. I watched as she painstakingly separated the layer of fat from the thin skin of the intestine as if she were pulling a label from its backing and discarded it. When the remaining intestines were translucent, she soaked them in detergent and thoroughly rinsed them. Then she boiled them with an onion, potato, and bay leaf for about ten hours. She warned me that the whole process took all day so you had to get up and start at dawn. I never forgot how to make them and have cleaned many a pot and served them over the years.

Despite my mother's and maternal grandmother's often voiced disdain for this food and their refusal to get involved in its preparation, if I cleaned and cooked them, they ate my chit'lins with gusto. I prepared a lot of them when we lived in the East Woodlawn and South Shore neighborhoods. In my memories, I always associate chit'lins with that part of my personal history and that part of Chicago even when I lived elsewhere in the country for almost two decades.

CHAPTER 13
GOODBYE TO PARKWAY

When I was about thirteen, my close friendship with Brenda collapsed with a bang after the "Campfire Girls" incident. The Campfire Girls organization was an older but lesser known version of the Girl Scouts and the only organized girls' group I knew of in Parkway. I joined at Brenda's invitation. Instead of Girl Scout green, we wore navy blue and orange. She and I were Bluebirds together--junior Campfire girls-- had camped out in Washington Park, and cooked and ate charred hotdogs and s'mores. We sold glazed doughnuts at the Greyhound Bus Station downtown to raise money for our troop, wove clumsy potholders from fabric strips, and made lumpy table mats from wet reeds and generally had a good time. I liked the other girls in the troop, too, although I didn't know them well, as they lived in Parkway units in the complexes on 64th or 66th streets and I saw them only at the meetings.

The last year I was in Campfire, my mother suddenly decided she would become the leader of our troop after the former one moved back to Alabama. After all, she reminded me, she had taught in public school and had even briefly taught tough Negro and Latino girls in a reform school on the West Side. She told me she was going to introduce the Parkway Campfire girls to sewing and clothing design since she sewed all our clothes. She brought some leftover fabric to her first meeting, along with needles, scissors, thread, and an easy pattern to teach us how to make a simple sleeveless summer top.

That year, Brenda had been growing wilder and bolder, or "faster", as the neighbors called girls who were sexually advanced or sassy-talking. Along with her huge fund of nasty stories and sexual references, she had developed an increasingly challenging and outright rebellious attitude towards most adults as well as other girls. Lately, she had been picking fights with me over everything and nothing or laughing at my homemade clothes which I already knew weren't hip. When I told her I was going to read *Gone with the Wind* after learning that the First Lady, Jackie Kennedy, had read it as a young girl, she mocked me, laughing, "You would be reading some old book! Who cares?!"

When Mother and I got to the Parkway clubhouse for the meeting, Brenda was already there, slouched in a folding chair next to her two new buddies--London Lawson, a cream-colored, puffy-lipped beauty with a long chestnut pageboy and sleepy eyes, and a scrawny girl with a weasely face named Norma something who had recently moved to Chicago from New York City. Norma and London always seemed to be looking for a fight, and it was rumored in the troop that they "did it" with boys. Mother introduced herself and started telling our group about the fun of making your own clothes, while, at the same time, Brenda, London and Norma started talking loudly to each other about some boys they knew. The rest of us sat and tried to listen politely to Mother but I could tell trouble was going to erupt any minute.

Mother ignored Brenda and her friends' noise and behavior, suggesting that we all go to the table to spread out the fabric and pin the pattern on it. Brenda jumped up and shouted, "You can't make us! I'm not sewing nothing! I don't want no homemade clothes." London and Norma joined in, refusing to go to the table. I noticed Brenda was wearing the latest: cat's-eye eyeliner, visible beneath her thick glasses, and platinum lipstick which I'd never seen on her before. Her hair was pinned in a high, sprayed beehive with French roll, not her usual pony tail braid. *When had she gotten so grown looking?* I wondered. Her eyes were angry but she was smirking. Then the insults started to fly back and forth. Brenda and London called Mother a bitch. Mother angrily called them "little heifers" and then, shouting, "little bitches!" I was appalled at what Brenda had started. I jumped up and shouted several times—"Stop talking that way to my mother, y'all." Everyone ignored me and continued the verbal abuse. In our neighborhood, the mere mention of someone's mother in a derogatory manner could get you beaten up or even killed. And when you talked to others' mothers, you said only, "Yes, ma'am, No ma'am." And, I was ashamed that Mother had instantly sunk to their level and cursed at them like some of the rowdier mothers in the complex or the teachers at St. Matt's. And then I was ashamed of being ashamed of her. I wanted her to remain dignified, yet I was mortified and angry that these girls had singled out my mother for this flash fire revolt. We'd had other leaders who'd been obeyed with never a harsh or insubordinate word.

I stood there transfixed with embarrassment and regret. Everyone was looking at me wondering what I was going to do. Explode? Beat up Brenda and the others? I didn't know myself what I should or could do. Physically, I couldn't fight three girls. Anyway, I wasn't the type to jump up and beat butts or start cursing. After my shouts were ignored, I fell mute, tongue-tied but livid, charged up but defeated. Suddenly, I just wanted to get out of there. Angry tears were starting to seep out of Mother's eyes. She stalked around the room aimlessly cursing, and then threw the fabric and scissors back in the box we'd brought. Brenda got bored and announced she was leaving, sauntering out with London and Norma scurrying along after her. I knew my relationship with Brenda was over. No matter how I craved friends and inclusion, I couldn't disregard or forgive this.

The Chit'lin Coast

As for Mother, she had never tried to hide her feelings about Brenda. She didn't like Brenda--thought her overly mature, controlling and mouthy--and Brenda knew it. What had made Mother think she could lead someone who was not only a budding leader herself but someone becoming notorious for being "grown" and defiant? On the other hand, what made Brenda decide to take on my mother? Although Mother didn't like her, she had always been polite to her and let us play together. It seemed as if every time I had a friendship something happened to destroy it. After Brenda and her posse left, the meeting broke up and the girls not involved fled. I wished I could have disappeared, too. I silently helped Mother load up the sewing stuff.

A few days later, Mother, still fuming, asked Brenda's mother to come over to the house to discuss the matter. I'd never seen Mrs. Jones off her couch or away from the TV. She came alone and sat quietly, with a sullen expression, while Mother complained about Brenda's behavior at the meeting. To make matters worse, Mother accused Brenda of stealing money from my piggybank. I had asked her not to do that. The truth is that Brenda had stolen the money a few weeks before although I'd decided to say nothing about it to her—-the pig didn't hold much money—-but Mother plowed on. Mrs. Jones jumped up suddenly and yelled, "I don't care what Brenda Jean said to you and I think Flowuz(that's how she pronounced my name) stole her own money." Mrs. Jones then marched out the door, banging it behind her.

I never went to a Campfire girls meeting again. I kicked myself out of the troop. I avoided Brenda, who never apologized or acknowledged me again, either. Just before we left Parkway for good, I saw London one day on the street. I was surprised when she stopped and said, head hanging, eyes downcast, that she was sorry she'd cursed at my mother: "I never talked like that to anyone's mother before and I'm sorry I did that." I didn't know what to say but just nodded numbly.

The last year we lived in Parkway, I thought I would miss the friendship I had with Brenda but I didn't. At thirteen, I spent a lot of time traveling to my faraway high school and doing homework. Then, in my sophomore year, we moved to Minerva Avenue in East Woodlawn, closer to Jackson Park and the lake. Brenda enrolled at the local public high school, Englewood, and, a couple years later, I bumped into some other girls I knew in Parkway, who told me she'd had a baby.

I was not the only one in our family with friendship problems. While we lived in Parkway, Mother was never friendly with the other mothers her age. She ignored them and they ignored her. Even when I thought I was tight friends with Brenda and before the Campfire Girls debacle, Mother would remark to me that her mother was particularly negligent and, frankly, ignorant. Mother arrived home every night utterly exhausted from the long bus ride from her West Side school assignment and excused her avoidance of the neighbors by claiming she had no time or energy to hobnob. The only women she occasionally got together with were her sisters or old friends from high school or college, who certainly didn't live in Parkway. Mother avoided even them much of time because they had married better than she had, had fewer kids, had beautiful homes, and might judge or pity her.

When I was about thirteen, she suddenly made a friend in one of the nearby apartments—-a Mrs. Jefferson who was in her late seventies. Mrs. Jefferson looked like someone in a 19th century photograph: center–parted iron gray hair drawn into a bun, high-necked blouse clasped with a cameo, and a grimly set mouth under a mannish black moustache. Her husband, who followed her around like a puppy, was a meek, tea-colored gentleman, silent, bent like a spoon, and trembling. Mrs. Jefferson could talk a streak, often lavishing praise on me as a beautiful young woman. Shy and insecure as I was, I didn't believe her. "You're a lovely young woman but don't ever be vain," she would admonish upon spotting me. Mother visited her often and I wondered what she and this woman could have had in common, until I discovered that, despite her age and gender, Mrs. Jefferson was the project's top bookie and gambler. Mother was a bookie's dream-—naïve and in need of money.

Mother had an elderly great uncle, Clarence, with whom she was very close. Knowing he was a widower who lived in rooming houses and ate at diners, she checked up on him often and took him peach cobblers sweetened with saccharine to accommodate his diabetes. When Clarence died, he left Mother $2,000, which Mrs. Jefferson told her she could double at the races. Mother, who always thought herself to be smarter and more sophisticated than our mostly southern-born neighbors, handed the entire amount over to the old woman, who not only pocketed or lost it but never spoke to Mother again. I didn't know about this until one afternoon I spotted Mother banging on the Jefferson's door begging the old woman to come out and talk to her. I ran up and pulled her off their steps, leading her by the hand, like a child, back to our apartment. With tears dripping down her face, Mother admitted to me, "She stole my little money."

I was frustrated and angry at Mother for giving the money to Mrs. Jefferson. I couldn't bring myself to comfort her and didn't speak to her for a few days. I was ashamed for Mother and hurt that she didn't think of us before handing her inheritance over to that old lady. I'd hoped that Clarence's money would be used to buy us all some new clothes or a trip somewhere. We'd never been anywhere but Michigan during the summers. We alternated between having no car and buying and riding in very old, very used cars. I'd just started high school and wanted to wear clothes that were "tough", the kids' word for cool, and not homemade. Like most teens, I thought I knew everything about everything. I didn't but I did know Mother had been a fool to trust Mrs. Jefferson.

When I finally calmed down enough to speak to Mother without being disrespectful, I scolded her, "Mother, we needed that money. Daddy only sends you sixty dollars a month for us. You should never have given that money to Mrs. Jefferson. She always seemed like a crook to me. You'll never get it back." I was right. We never saw that $2,000 again. This was not the first or last time I questioned my mother's judgment, but it was the first time I felt I should start watching what she did, a feeling that never left me, thereafter, and, unfortunately, became eminently justified. It was one of the first times I felt as if I was a grown woman in some way. I could see Mrs. Jefferson was a phony while my mother could not. And this betrayal, along with the Brenda debacle, taught me something about friendships, their pitfalls and effect on my ability to trust others.

Although we didn't live in Parkway longer than anywhere else, it was there I stopped being a little girl and started becoming a young woman physically (I started menstruating) and mentally (I started getting what life was: good/bad/up/down but, most of all, uncertain.

CHAPTER 14
HIGH SCHOOL HELL

I started high school when I was barely thirteen. After the salutatorian/valedictorian debacle at St. Matt's, I was ready to go. High school seemed like an exciting, if terrifying, new frontier and an escape from the dead-end learning experience of St. Matt's. Most of the other girls in Parkway attended the nearest public high school, Englewood, or one of the few dying all-girl Catholic schools on the South Side like St. Elizabeth's, Mercy, or Academy of Our Lady. Mother, still in competitive mode with her better married and incomed sisters, pushed her budget to the limit and decided to send me to the high school-—Divine Providence High School--run by the same denomination as St. Matt's. That wasn't her only motive—she had been told by my teachers over the years I was bright and she wanted me to have the best education possible. She was also college-educated and wanted to make sure I was headed that way and didn't get "bogged down with babies and a dog of a husband", as she put it.

The high school I went to was on the city's white, southwest edge, across from the suburb of Evergreen Park, Illinois and not far from a popular picnic ground, the Dan Ryan Forest Preserve. We lived on the black southeast side near the lake first on South Parkway and then Minerva. The South Side is so vast that to get there I had to take an hour-long bus ride up 63rd street to Kedzie and transfer to a buzzing and sparking streetcar to 87th and Kedzie.

While on the 63rd street bus, I always looked for the corner of Carpenter and 63rd, because of a childhood memory. When I was about eight, my father and a couple of uncles had driven around in Englewood looking for a frame two-flat to buy. In those days, the streets and neighborhoods going west on 63rd were populated predominantly by working class whites, but for some reason, Dad had decided to defy them and move there. I was in the car with my dad, his brothers and one of their wives that day when we got caught in a flash mini-riot at Carpenter supposedly ignited because some whites had spotted Negroes, like us, looking at homes and driving around in the area. I remembered the inflamed faces and the angry shouts of the whites lining the curb, surrounding our car, banging on the hood, and terrifying me. I remembered Uncle Mac's wife beating on the back of Dad's seat and begging him "Let me out! I'm gonna fight these white trash bastards! I'm gonna beat somebody's ass!" I was relieved when my father, ignoring her, turned the car sharply and we sped away from Englewood.

When I waited for those streetcars to the high school at 63rd and Kedzie, it seemed as if it were always winter, and winters were colder in those days. I froze waiting for those streetcars. The bus drivers for the 63rd street leg were easygoing young black guys, but the Kedzie streetcars were manned by crusty older white drivers who closed the doors on me before I got fully aboard or, if they were waiting for their scheduled departure time, kept the doors closed so I couldn't sit down and get warm before they departed from the bus barn.

To make matters worse, the ovens of the Nabisco factory on that corner chugged out nauseating burned sugar smoke that made me sick to my unbreakfasted stomach. One day, it was so cold and the streetcar was so long in coming that when it finally arrived and I climbed in, my knees locked and I fell face forward. I hit the floor with a bang broken only by my hands. With stinging hands and raw knees, I pushed myself up and gathered my scattered school papers. No one helped me up. The fat, flushed-face driver looked stonily forward. I heard sniggers and guffaws from the white boys, ducktailed hair greased to a mirror shine, who always seemed to be sitting at the backs of those buses.

Before starting this school, the only contact I had with it was when St. Matt's competed there in religious choral contests against other all-white elementary schools, in the same denomination. For weeks prior to the contests, our black teachers would gravely lecture us about "acting our age and not our color" in front of the white students and teachers. Miss Plymouth warned us that, in being obstreperous, we would demonstrate just why "white folks don't want us around." More attention was paid to our not embarrassing our race than to our singing. She also warned us that students who acted out in any way during the contests would be expelled if their antics embarrassed the teachers in front of the white folks. When we practiced marching in the processionals into the auditorium that began the competitions, Miss Plymouth quickly moved the fairest-complexioned girls with the longest, silkiest hair to the front of the choral line, because she was sure they'd make the best first impression.

I half listened, as I always did, to these frequent lectures about "correct" Negro student behavior. Miss Plymouth didn't have to worry about me. I was shy and the last thing I would ever do was draw negative or positive attention to myself in front of my classmates, teachers and a faceless crowd of whites. When we piled out of the school bus at the choral meets, I felt as if I were walking on egg shells. Miss Plymouth expected us to be the best singers as well as credits to our race. We were supposed to ignore our competitors whispering "nigger, nigger, nigger" when we stood in the hall waiting to march in. When we complained to Miss Plymouth about the taunts, she'd either deny they'd been made or say, "Just ignore them and concentrate on your singing." As if I could. I was such a nervous wreck before, during and after these meets I couldn't eat or sleep. When our group marched in singing *O Come All Ye Faithful* or *O Holy Night,* I'd lock my knees to keep them from shaking while I walked.

I really became a basket case after I became a high school student there. My class of blacks was not the first at D.P. (that's what we called it), as there had been a smattering of black students earlier. With one or two exceptions, however, those blacks had transferred to other high schools after having had their fill of hostility, ostracism, and ridicule. In my class, there were nine black females but no black males. Every day started the same—with mocking hoots, laughs, and chimp noises as we boarded the bus. Whooping boys in letter jackets balled up potato chip and Twinkie wrappers and catapulted them towards our faces. Loud whispers of "Go back to Africa" could be heard over the transistorized sound of Frankie Valli wailing *Big Girls Don't Cry.* I sat at the front of the bus, back rigid, head down, or I looked straight out the window. I always sat on the edge of my seat as if poised for flight. I tried always to have a book to stare at even if I was too nervous to read. Darcy, one of my few black classmates who rode the same route, and I never looked at the back rows no matter what sounds we heard. One day after riding the same buses but not sitting together for several tense months, Darcy whispered, looking scared, "We should always sit together." I looked at those catcalling white boys in the back when she said that and saw smirking faces that did not bother to hide their hatred and rage. I thought if the two of us were always together, at least on the bus, maybe it wouldn't be so bad. I quickly agreed: "Okay."

When we arrived at the school, we jumped off the bus, race-walked with heads down, looking neither to the right or left and headed straight for our lockers. It made it a bit easier to pretend you couldn't see or hear anything. Smaller than its public counterparts, the high school was a lonely blonde brick slab on the corner of a field facing a bleak cemetery and flanked by a blinking radio tower.

The Chit'lin Coast

Every day, Darcy and I would deposit our books and coats in our lockers while ignoring the words "niggers" and "apes" some phantom scrawled overnight on those lockers, no matter how many times we erased them. Darcy and I were not really friends nor were we friends with the other blacks, but we bonded because we had to. We sat with the other black girls in a cluster at the front or side of our home room instinctively avoiding the back seats where the most hostile group sat, their legs stuck out to trip the unwary. In homeroom and in other classes, paper wads hit the backs of our heads when the teacher wasn't looking, as well as when the teacher was looking. After school, when Darcy and I or one of the others walked to the bus stop we narrowly missed being deliberately hit by guys vrooming out of the parking lot.

Most of our teachers were ministers who talked all the time about the sins of divorce and dancing but never saw guys aiming pencils at our eyes. We attended classes where we were never called on or where we received C's for A work. When we received A's from a few teachers, we were refused membership in the National Honor Society Chapter because we were told "It isn't time," or as one teacher told me, "The honor society never got back to me on that." There were classmates who never spoke to us, looked past or through us, snickered or wrenched away when we spoke or passed them. We were spoken to or befriended (school only, no home visitation, please) only by those white students who also didn't fit in— too fat, dumb, funny-looking, handicapped, poor, foreign or weird. We blacks got supposedly well-meaning comments from even these misfits—

"My parents hate colored people, but I told them you seem okay", or "If there's one thing my dad can't stand it's colored people and Japs 'cause he fought them in the war", or "Do you live in the same neighborhood as our cleaning lady?", or, after my weekend visit to Miss Suzy Q's Beauty Parlor for a press and curl: "You Negroes' hair is always fuzzy. What did you do to get it to lay down?"

Every Tuesday morning we lined up for a mandatory hour-long religious assembly. There was always a brief sermon by visiting ministers who scornfully lambasted Catholics for supposedly believing that good works and praying to saints would get you into heaven. Eyes raised to the heavens, they piously insisted that Catholics would go to hell for not just believing in Jesus alone. These sermons were generic in substance and quality. They never dealt with real vice--drugs/prostitution, specific societal evils or injustices like intolerance or discrimination nor acknowledged or addressed the sweeping changes (racial and gender equality, the war) which were even then knocking at our country's door. I daydreamed through these sermons. It was the one hour of silence in the school. No one could call you "nigger" there.

Gym class was the absolute worst as far as I was concerned. I was mortified at displaying my flat chest and stick-legged body in the showers, but most of all I dreaded the square dancing semester. At this school, dancing was equated with fornication, which, according to the minister-teachers at the school, was the most evil thing one could do in life. These ministers harshly condemned fornication and sex itself except after marriage and for procreation purposes only. However, although dancing was flat out sinful, square dancing, part of the regular gym curriculum, was the inexplicable and puzzling exception.

During the square dancing classes, our gym teachers partnered each female dancer with a male. The teachers, a buxom farm-girl blonde and a mannish, wiry brunette, shouted the dance commands as if we were at an exciting barn dance, "Allemande left with your right hand! Swing your partner, right and left grand!" or something like that. That should have worked well but square dancing required touching when executing the swings, do-si-dos, allemande rights and lefts. The white boys in the class all refused to touch us black girls. They accompanied their refusals with loud "icks", "yecchs", hand wiping, and cracks about dancing with monkeys. "Hey," Miss Kepler, the muscle-bound brunette yelled at us black girls in her adenoidal voice,

"You gals, you, Kim, Diamond, and Juanita aren't making the dances work! I could flunk you for that!" One day a boy escalated his refusal to touch me to a higher level. Instead of merely dramatically backing away from me or wiping his hand if it touched me, he stood in the middle of the room and refused to dance at all. "Go stand on the side," twittered the farm girl teacher, gesturing the guy to the wall. The dancing continued while both female gym teachers blithely ignored the boy's behavior, and called the dance moves as if everyone were dancing merrily and cooperatively. Neither the grandstanding boy nor the other boys were ever punished, or even reprimanded, for refusing to dance nicely or touch us.

After that standoff, I was clumsily paired with a fellow who got around touching me by pretending he was dancing alone, allemanding and do-si-doing by himself. I felt like dirt, as if it was my fault not only that he wouldn't dance with me but that I was born part of a group everyone was entitled to hate.

At the end of freshman year, at least three black girls who entered with me left for public schools. One of the girls, Cassie, had graduated with me from the eighth grade, so I knew her well enough to ask her why she was jumping ship.

"Girl, I can't stand any more of the shit here and my mother told me I don't have to!" What could I say? I agreed with and envied her.

The years passed but nothing substantially changed about my life at high school. After finishing the assigned homework in study hall, I read the entire works of Agatha Christie, never lifting my eyes. Once, I asked a beefy duck-tail at my assigned study table for the time and he responded by telling me to shut my black mouth. My smiling and jocular sophomore speech teacher, a new arrival from Washington state, referred to Jim, Huck's friend, as a kind "darky" when we were discussing *Huckleberry Finn*. When I was a senior and visited our usually deserted career counseling office I was told by the part-time minister and career counselor that I should look into truck-driving opportunities. Instead of a prom, since dancing was so sinful, an annual banquet was held. It was as anticipated and planned-for by the girls as carefully as a traditional prom, including dates with tuxedoed boys, long, pastel dresses, corsages and boutonnieres. No black girls were invited or attended, as far as I know, in any of the four years of my high school life.

The cafeteria was like a zoo at lunch time. If we blacks went to the counters for chips or pie to go with our brown-bag lunches, legs shot out to trip us. Food and garbage were thrown at us and around our table. We couldn't escape because of an iron-clad policy preventing students from leaving the school or even the lunchroom. We couldn't sit in the study hall and escape the torment because small school that it was, the cafeteria was also the study hall.

When we looked at the garbage-throwing ring leaders, they whooped and chattered like apes, dangling their arms near the floor and scratched their thighs as gorillas and chimps supposedly do. One day, a short, red-faced freshman boy who looked more like a third grader threw a carton of milk in my face. "Yah! nigger!" he shouted to raucous laughter from his table. Although we had never retaliated or even defended ourselves in the past, I saw red, jumped up and picked up one of the heavy cafeteria chairs even though I was a skinny couch potato. I brought it down on his back. He yelped and tried to run. Before I could truly kick his ass(I was that mad), the teacher monitoring the cafeteria, a bony acne-scarred fellow, ran over. "You, two stop that fighting! Go to the principal's office at once!"

The principal, built like a stone-faced block of wood, threatened us both, "I oughta expel the two of you. No, don't tell me who did what. I don't care. Now go back to your class and act like Christians!" I still felt I had to try to explain. I was shaking from the adrenaline and the injustice of it all. Plus, I believed the little jerk would do this again if not punished.

"Mr. Gordon, I stuttered, he does this every.." "Not another word!" Gordon barked, staring straight over our heads, "March on back there and I don't want to see either of you in here again!"

When I returned to the cafeteria, drained and bodily sore, one of the other black girls, Cathy, radiating embarrassment, asked me,

"Why did you do that?" When she asked me that, I realized my mother was right: you could not always depend on other Negroes to support you if it involved fighting with whites.

Even when there were not personal attacks, we were always outsiders. There were defined cliques as there are everywhere. There was the cheerleader/prom queen/quarterback/class president clique. The girls had straight, blonde hair and blue eyes. The mostly brunette guys were tall and lean. Both the girls and guys had cars, sharp clothes and decent but not outstanding grades. There was the second-tier clique, all of whom dressed like and hung around the first group and kissed their asses in an attempt to be popular, too. There were the outlaws-—slouching washroom smokers, mini-skirt and heavy-eyeliner wearers, girls who chattered incessantly about making out with guys, dudes who had cigarettes hanging out of their mouths and pocket combs stuck in their hair. Then there was a clique, if you wanted to call it that, of the outcasts: big brains, pimples, mossy or picket fence teeth, fat or skinny asses, disabilities. We weren't part of any clique unless you call sitting with the other blacks at all times, whether you liked them or not, to constitute a clique. Looking at the pecking order from any angle, we were last.

I moped around the house when I wasn't at school, brooding about the school. Between my junior and senior years, Mother decided my problem wasn't the school but that I lacked what she called "poise". According to her, she worked with other Negro women whose teenage daughters were well-groomed, refined, intelligent, cheerful, and who beat mobs of boyfriends away from their doors. I came home from school one day to overhear her tell her sister on the phone, "Flower is so clumsy and awkward. She's got a bad attitude all the time. I'm going to send her to charm school." Charm schools were very popular in the black sections of the South Side of Chicago in the 50's and 60's. The idea was that Negro girls should be trained to be as graceful, polite and lady-like as white women supposedly were and, thus, to counteract our so-called deficits—-our "bad" hair, "liver" lips, big butts, brash or surly manners. I was humiliated by my mother's words and defiant, but she won. The summer between my junior and senior year, I was forced to attend the Miss Debonaire Charm School held in a 63rd street storefront. Frannie, the instructor, was cute and curvaceous but struggling with vitiligo – the loss of melanin in her skin. I hung out with one girl, Kay, who seemed to already to be "charmed"—-she was fair-skinned, had a long brown pony-tail and a publicly sweet manner. Behind Frannie's back, though, Kay called her "Elsie" or mooed slyly because her skin was spotted like a milk cow's. Kay held an amused and mocking contempt for the "charm" process and students. She and I spent the whole summer at charm school walking around balancing books on our heads, supposedly to improve our posture, learning to cross our legs at the ankles and not the knees, and laughing at the other girls who took the "lessons" seriously.

The charm school had no great short or long term effect on me, but Mother seemed satisfied that I had been transformed from an ugly duckling to a swan and stopped commenting on my gauche manner and appearance.

We black girls at the high school pretended or perhaps truly disdained rah-rah school activities like homecoming and school trips. But in our senior year, we decided to attend the homecoming game, since this was our last year, and because Anita, a black girl (albeit an exotic and agile one), had finally penetrated the cheerleader ranks. One of the other girls who had attended the same grammar school as I, said to me, defensively, "I hate this place (she always called D.P. 'the place' or 'this place'). I'm only going to that game to support Anita."

I couldn't even say that. I wasn't sure whether Anita, who'd also gone to elementary school with us, cared about my support or not. But, I'd never, ever admit to this girl, who was always critical of me, that I was going because for once I just wanted to feel like I was in high school. At the game, we were careful not to cheer for "our" team.

Our silence meant not showing any enthusiasm for the school in any way, shape or fashion—-not that anyone seemed to care. After the game, the floats moved slowly past us as we huddled in a bundled-up clump on the outer edges of the bleachers. The floats carried several shivering but cheerfully waving cheerleaders, the homecoming queen, her court and their football player escorts. I didn't see Anita anywhere during the game or the parade. When the game was over, the white students jumped in their GTOs and split for a homecoming party. Feeling deflated and somewhat cheated, I followed the other black girls and we boarded the northbound or eastbound buses headed back to the southeast side and home.

In our senior year, four of us girls flouted the tradition of blacks ignoring events at the school even when we were not actually or subtly barred. We went on the senior trip to Washington, DC. None of us had ever been there nor had our parents, so we eagerly anticipated the trip, even though it was by train and we had been warned that the District of Columbia was still officially segregated in places.

We rode the train to DC in our usual brown female knot. Though we'd not been personally or emotionally close at school, we did everything together on this trip. We roomed together and rode the bus together to see the sights. We ate at the cafeteria stops and at a dinner at a Virginia inn together. We got sick of one another eventually (or at least I did) but I think each silently came to the conclusion we had no alternative but to stick together. The school arranged an amusement park tour one night which culminated in a dance on a riverboat on the Potomac. Apparently, dancing wasn't sinful at night in another city on a boat. We attended the dance and sat self-consciously on the sidelines watching one of the most popular girls from our school dance with and later leave with a teenaged guy from a sister school. While our white classmates were frugging to the Beach Boys *Sloop John B*, we heard a boy, from another school ask one of our female classmates who we were. The answer—-"Just some Negroes who go to our school".

During the four years, I complained often to Mother about life at the school. I told her about the Harold sisters who cried every day because their mother wouldn't let them transfer. Mother responded by pointing out the cost of the school---if it was expensive it was good--and the supposed excellence of the education I was receiving. She interrupted my tales of tripping, food-throwing and name-calling to remind me that she integrated a white South Side public high school—Calumet High School--in the 40's.

"Oh, Flower, it was horrible," she would counter. "The white kids at Calumet were so dirty, so low-down. Those kids and their parents rioted, threw rocks and cursed at me. They started all that ugly shit over one little black girl, me. And I was all by myself. The police escorted me to the school door, but I could tell they didn't want to. Mama and Daddy couldn't do anything about it. I was so sorry that I had transferred from Lucy Flower," the all-female vocational school she had attended with her sisters.

I never could tell if she felt my experiences weren't as bad as hers or if she believed integration experiences were always awful, so I should toughen up. Her stories of what she endured made me feel guilty for whining about what was happening at my high school. Besides, she claimed that girls at the public high schools had babies in the washrooms—a sure sign of a poor educational environment. She asked me, "Do you want to be around that?" Of course I didn't. Her attitude was one I observed in most black adults I had spoken to. They never uttered the word "integration", and "diversity" was an unknown term but it was clear they believed it was imperative that we blacks, as a group, be fully included in mainstream American life. Anyone venturing into the white world could expect and suffer danger, pain, rejection, because that's just the way it was.

I'd be lying if I said I never had a white friend at this school. There was one girl who seemed to be in all of my classes. She ended up sitting next to me in my freshman classes and as the years passed, we often chose to sit together. She was plumply blonde, milk-maid pretty, and had a single mother like mine (hers was widowed) and, also, not much money. Our lives seemed similar in many ways. Neither of us was popular. We laughed together, compared class notes, partnered on projects, and chuckled at the wanna-bes—those second-tier classmates who endlessly sucked up to the top tier. During our senior year, this friend suddenly became popular with the cheerleader crowd. I don't know how or why, as she always said the popular kids rejected her because she didn't come from money, had no daddy, and wasn't pretty enough. I was surprised she had clicked with this crowd but didn't feel left out until she announced to me one day, giddy with happiness that she was having a pajama party the next weekend and her guest list included the most popular girls. I kept my face blank when she told me this. As a Negro you never showed, if you could help it, how exclusion made you feel. She must have seen something in my face that gave her pause, because she then said quickly and casually, "No, you can't come, sorry. My mother doesn't like Negroes." I said nothing at the time (what could I say?) but didn't chat easily and freely with her after that. About a week after graduation, I received a letter from her announcing that we would be best friends forever. She didn't mention the pajama party. According to her letter, she supposedly valued my friendship very much. I pitched the letter in the wastebasket unanswered. That was that as far as I was concerned.

    I stayed in a constant fog of anxiety, depression, and fear for almost the entire four years at the school, and it adversely affected my physical and mental health. Sometime in my second year, I developed intense leg and lower abdominal aches of unknown origin that wouldn't go away. I went to a couple of doctors who couldn't figure out what was wrong. My mother finally found a doctor who was known for selling gym and work excuses. He solemnly diagnosed me as having an "open spinal" condition and gave me a letter excusing me from gym. I never went to gym class again. Miraculously, my pains decreased and then vanished. During my sophomore year, I got a raging case of pleurisy and pneumonia, involving frightening non-stop nosebleeds, excruciating backaches, vomiting, and breathing difficulty. The symptoms got worse at school, and one day I was sent home. I was still going to my old pediatrician, Dr. Bell, who scolded my mother for not getting me treated earlier, suggesting that I could have died. Neither my mother nor I made a connection between my illness and the school atmosphere at the time, but even sick as I was, I was happy because I didn't have to attend school for two weeks.

At the time, I believed that my mother ignored or downplayed all my symptoms because she thought children were never seriously ill. In reality, she was probably just facing the fact that all doctor visits had to be paid for with cash on the barrelhead. Pre-paid health insurance was an unknown. As far as mental anguish or stress was concerned, in those days if something concerned, depressed, or scared you, you were supposed to suck it up. There were no anti-depressants, tranquilizers, counselors, or therapists to ameliorate your troubles--at least not in my world. If there was little money to pay for physical ailments there was certainly none for "head" treatments. No one in our community or family thought such help had any value, and seeking it was regarded as shameful. Black people weren't supposed to be "crazy"--there was no time or money for that. Psychotherapy was an indulgence and the province of white folks. If you were grown, drinking might make you feel better, at least temporarily, but if you were not old enough to drink, you simply had to outgrow your troubled reaction to the ways of the world.

I found no comfort in religion. Even though I attended parochial schools, we were not an authentically religious family. The religious schools were a device my mother used to provide me with the supposedly superior education they offered. There was no concentrated or public focus by the media, academia or political leaders on the phenomena or psychology of discrimination or bullying and their effects on children and teens. Most people just stood up to bullies or ran away from them. My unhappiness with the racial atmosphere at my school was regarded by my family and other blacks as the cloak of misery every black person was forced to wear.

My head pounded and stomach churned every morning before school and I had to literally force myself to get up and go although the bus rides became easier. During my junior year, another girl who'd also gone to St. Matt's, started riding the same bus. Je t'aime was a Negro princess. An only child, she had long and incredibly thick and rich auburn hair and green eyes. Her parents openly adored and praised her—"My mother told me I'm the best thing that ever happened to her" she said--and she carried herself with total confidence. She had a sardonic sense of humor and didn't seem to let what I considered to be the abundant racism at the school bother her. She was a calming influence on me and made the journey there a bit more bearable. Although she was a couple of years younger, we were also friends outside school. She didn't live far from me and her home, a neat one-family graystone was definitely enviable. Her stylish mother's cooking was superb. I first tasted scalloped oysters, rich and creamy under a cracker crust as well as paprika chicken at her table.

My senior year went better then prior years, possibly because the white students had become used to our presence, but also because, black or white, we were looking outward, excited about leaving, going to college or new jobs. There were even several girls who were getting married. Our attention had drifted away from the school and each other.

I felt better about myself, too. After charm school ended, I got my hair cut in a popular style, gave myself nightly Noxzema facials, and started wearing heavy eye makeup which made me feel more hip and mature. Other kids at school commented on my improved appearance and more and more I started thinking of myself as a potential and presentable college student.

Between 1962 and 1966, the civil rights and anti-war movements grew progressively more powerful, visible, and forceful in American life and politics. But my high school was curiously and hermetically sealed insofar as these outside elements or events were concerned. Social movements were never mentioned by faculty or students publicly in my memory.

"President John F. Kennedy has just been assassinated. Please get your hats and coats. School is dismissed for the day," our principal boomed in somber tones over the intercom system. I was a sophomore sitting in biology class and I was stunned, disbelieving and disoriented. Like everyone else, I numbly got my coat and left that November day in 1963. I walked to the bus stop in a daze and rode home in a fog, but I still noticed the sky was pewter and stormy and hung so low it seemed to skim the tops of our heads. The pall of the assassination hung over the nation for months and, in fact, still haunts and mystifies many who were alive then. Although several of the upper class girls ran around the halls screaming and crying that the Communists had killed Kennedy, thereafter his death was never mentioned again by any student or teacher in my presence. It was as if it had never happened or didn't affect our lives at all.

When Kennedy's successor, President Lyndon Johnson, squared off for the presidency against Republican Senator Barry Goldwater, the students seemed apathetic and indifferent to the race. There was one exception—a chubby, pink-cheeked, very blonde fellow in my class who walked around most of 1964 with a Goldwater button, the size of a sundial on his shirt which declared: "In your heart you know he's right." This was the same boy who told me one day in study hall, his tone dripping condescension, that he didn't know why folks were so hard on the Third Reich. After all, according to him, the horrible things that were done were perpetrated by "just a few criminals."

We weren't indifferent to politics in my house. Mother and I distributed leaflets and pamphlets for Johnson's re-election in our neighborhood. We were naïve about politics in many ways but believed at that time, if we were ever going to get our rights as full citizens of this country it would be by electing Democrats.

I concluded, ultimately, that my main goal was to survive my high school experience and go to college, where everything would be okay. My daily prayer was crude and simple: "Let this be over. Let me get out of here, Lord." College was a castle, a beacon of light shining in the distance as I stumbled unhappily toward it.

CHAPTER 15
65TH AND MINERVA

When I was almost fourteen, we moved to 65th and Minerva in East Woodlawn, even closer to the lake and Hyde Park--the glistening neighborhood of our teenage dreams. The block was a mix of well-kept, old-fashioned frame houses and scrupulously maintained two or six flats. Capping the northern end of the block was what they called a flatiron building—one shaped like an old-fashioned iron. The bus stop at the southern end of Minerva and 67th street faced a gloomy and deserted cemetery, Oak Woods. The neighbors all said that Negroes were barred from burial on its grounds, even though the cemetery was in a black neighborhood. This led my mother to remark, "They don't want us near them even when they're dead."

Although I never saw anyone readily recognizable as a prostitute or pimp, the flat-iron building was nicknamed the "pimp and ho' hotel" supposedly because prostitution was rampant in the building. Diagonally across from that hotel was what everyone called the "Mexican Building", because Puerto Ricans lived there. Ignorant of the differences between the various Spanish–speaking and Latino groups, everyone in our building and neighborhood called anyone who spoke Spanish a Mexican.

Our building was the largest on our block, centered like a jewel in the crown, a stately graystone with enormous breezy high ceilinged apartments with, to my delight, ceiling-high built-in bookshelves. The building was a co-op, where the residents owned their apartments. Mrs. Davis, our stooped eighty year-old neighbor proudly told us the moment she met us that the apartments had previously belonged to distinguished Jewish professors at the University of Chicago. As I was climbing the stairs shortly after we moved in, another neighbor, Mrs. Crawford(whose husband committed suicide while we lived there), sprang out of her door, hands on hips, curlers tight on her head. "I just wanted to tell you this was a nice building and block with famous Jewish professors until these low-life colored folks moved in," she declared emphatically.

We sublet our apartment from one of Mother's fellow teachers, who owned it but had returned to Ohio to take care of family business. The other owners, like Mrs. Davis and Mrs. Crawford, were elderly, determinedly middle class and very "seditty"-- blacks who were ghetto raised and still located but snobbish toward other blacks. They were not happy to see my single mother with her two noisy young sons and rather surly teenage daughter. It was immediately clear that they disapproved of us, so we ignored them as best we could. We focused on our happiness at leaving Parkway and the relative grandeur of the building. My joy was compounded by the fact we now lived about two blocks from the incredibly well-stocked Woodlawn Public Library and a couple of blocks from the Jackson Park el line. Ecstatically, I visited the library every week. I'd discovered mysteries, and it had the largest collection of golden-age mystery authors I'd seen. I wallowed in Agatha Christie, Ellery Queen and John Dickson Carr locked room whodunits. They were a delicious contrast to the stuffy classics we were assigned at school, such as *Moby Dick* and *Lord Jim*—-my personal least favorites. They also helped take my mind off the bleakness of the high school experience.

We had owned pets in Parkway but they were always java temple birds with pink beaks and feet(always named L'Oiseau) or goldfish(always named Gillian) purchased at Woolworth's. These pets were fine but hard to feel personally attached to. One day, after moving to Minerva, a stray cat left a litter of black and white kittens on the porch. When she returned, she took all but one. We took that kitten in and Kitty, the only name she would answer to, became what I considered my first real pet. Kitty wasn't cuddlesome or pretty but she was efficient. She arrived in the nick of time. Although the building had a grand façade and gorgeous rooms, mice scrambled endlessly through the walls of the building. We had started putting out poison on crackers for them but the poison emitted a sinister yellow smoke and smelled lethal. We were more afraid of it than the mice and so we stopped using it. However, we discovered when Kitty wasn't out in the alley getting impregnated, she was a born hunter. The mice we would surprise on our stove or counters when we first moved in vanished when the adult Kitty started catching them.

CHAPTER 16
MR. WEST AGAIN

About this time, my mother started disappearing at times after dinner and always on weekend mornings, for hours, and leaving Mr. West in charge. Yes, West was back. We hadn't seen him for several years and had just about forgotten him. I was displeased to see him—-he hadn't changed a bit, physically or mentally, but was in fact even stranger. Mother acted as if he had never disappeared and seemed welcoming. Later, when I grew up, I came to believe that perhaps she disappeared because she just wanted some time away from her children and responsibilities. She was a substitute teacher at rundown schools in depressed neighborhoods and always fretted about the defiant and dangerous kids she had to work with. After battling those kids all day, she came home to more kids---—me and my brothers.

All I knew, though, at that time, was that West started showing up every night and some mornings with a list he had written out, with my mother's approval, chores to be done---—mopping floors, dusting, and including onerous jobs like washing blinds and defrosting the refrigerator. He alternately screamed and hollered at me and my brothers, spit spraying from the space where his front tooth used to hang, demanding that we do the listed tasks and do them properly. Over and over he yelled, "Your mother put me in charge! You kids do your tasks and help your mother!"

West didn't do any of the listed chores himself although, after we'd finished, he swiped his fingers around the tables and floors checking for left-behind dirt, to my intense irritation. When we had finished to his satisfaction--a long haul—-he would demand that we flip channels on the tv (which he seemed afraid to operate) until we found the Divorce Court show he was addicted to. He spent the Divorce Court hour, mouth open, hanging on every word. Despite the show's colorless judges and stiff trial re-enactments, West was totally mesmerized by it. Although we knew the correct channel or could have found it in the TV Guide, we tormented him. We used our pliers(all the knobs had fallen off the TV)and purposely turned to wrong stations, making him miss most of the show. He retaliated by screaming louder about our undone or sloppily done chores and tattling to our mother when she finally returned. I was frustrated and disgusted. The minute he came in the door, I wanted him to leave.

Mother was quite talkative on most subjects but said nothing when we complained about West even when I asked her bluntly why she was leaving us with him so often.

"We can do the list without him, Mama. Why does he get to boss us when you're gone? I'm in high school! We don't need him."

We really did not need a baby-sitter. I had been sporadically baby-sitting for my brothers since I was eight and for others since I was eleven. Most parents thought since I could remember to lock the door with my latch key when I came home from school, make and receive calls politely, warm up soup and make sandwiches, refuse to open the door to strangers and work cheap, I was as good as it got.

Ever resistant to authority and generally sick of West and of Mother's lack of response to my complaints, I decided that he would have to go and I would have to make it happen. I had

The Chit'lin Coast

protested to Mother about his bossy ways and the frequent hissy fits he threw over missed dust or crooked bed making. Mother always responded vaguely, "He's helping me. I need help with raising three kids by myself." Sometimes, she would say, "I helped him when he got out of that hospital and didn't have a job and now he's helping me."

One Saturday morning, West hollered especially loudly at me for not throwing out some mop water and I decided the time had come for him to go. Incensed, I shouted back at him, "You're not my father, I don't have to do what you say. You know what? I'm going to tell my father on you. When he finds out that you've been coming up here, ordering us around when my mother's not here, he's going to kill you. And there won't be nothing Mother can do about it. She might want you around but we hate you! And, don't ask us to find Divorce Court on TV for you any more either!"

I kicked the bucket viciously, soaking West's run-over shoes and tide-water pants with dirty mop suds. Even though I was boiling mad, I knew I was taking a calculated risk in assuming my parents would be responsive. Daddy seemed indifferent to me and my brothers' everyday school or life problems although in the early years after their divorce, he had physically fought with Mother when he found out about her infrequent dates. Mother acted willfully unaware of West's most extreme behavior and omnipresence, always stressing that he was "helping" her.

I realized, deep down, I just wasn't quite nasty or sophisticated enough to concoct a detailed and believable sexual molestation or assault accusation although I realized that would be the most effective ploy. Even Dad would probably use such an accusation as a reason to beat up Mother and West--not really what I wanted. I just wanted West gone. I decided to make it seem as if West had done something so awful, so traumatizing that there would be no possible reason to keep him around. I would pretend that this "something" was so upsetting I couldn't describe it in specifics or talk about it.

When Mother returned from one of her mystery trips that afternoon, West and I both vaulted for the door, each wildly blaming the other for the fight we had while she was gone. West: "Rachel, she's bad. She threw mop water on my pants. She wouldn't finish mopping."

Me, crying: "Mama, he did something bad to me. I'm telling Daddy on him. Tell him, he can't come around here anymore."

Mother looked conflicted, which pissed me off. Who was the daughter and who was the old, scuzzy semi-boyfriend, here? I cried harder and thought: *I am the daughter. Shouldn't I come first? What's the matter with her?* I realized I hadn't had taken time to mess up my clothes or physically mark myself in some way. Despite my wild crying, I knew I didn't look or act sincerely distressed or as if I had been physically attacked. But looking at Mother's frown, I knew she would be worried about whether the authorities or Dad would find out she'd left her adolescent daughter alone numerous times with an unstable grown man.

Although I hadn't dared tell Mike and Eric my plan to get West kicked out—I didn't think I could trust them to shut up about it--they surprisingly played along. Eric was silent and big-eyed while I yelled about West. Mike, pointed at West and said, "He did something to Kim. I'm telling Daddy."

I thought—*thank God for them—for once!*

Looking at the floor, Mother whispered: "Joe, you're going to have to leave and not come back."

West started sobbing. "Rachel, you need me. You need me to help you. You're struggling to raise three kids alone." "I know Joe, you've helped me but she is my daughter," Mother muttered, throwing me a hard to read look.

When Mother turned away, I stood, arms crossed, smiling a small evil smile when West finally looked up at me. He trudged to the closet, got out his Salvation Army-purchased coat, and slowly put it on. He tried to plead with Mother some more but she abruptly and silently cut him off and flung open the door. He went out still crying loudly.

At first, after the incident, Mother had little to say to me about anything. I felt that she knew I had lied and manipulated a situation to get rid of West, but that she couldn't do anything about it. I was her daughter and it wouldn't look right to have taken his side. We never did discuss the situation or the incident. Neither Mike nor I told Daddy about it as we had threatened. Mother, for her part, never asked me what West had supposedly done to me that was so awful nor did she ask to see any evidence of West's wrongdoing. I was glad since I would have had to invent something, but I also wondered what kind of mother wouldn't ask. *What if I had been raped and was too ashamed to discuss it? Why doesn't she ask?* I asked myself this over and over.

Even with Mother's strange and unsatisfactory reaction to the supposed incident, I felt tremendously relieved after West was kicked out. I suppressed all thoughts about what I knew had been my selfishness and dishonesty. I was delighted not to see him around and not at all sorry that my mother was out a boyfriend. It had been hard for me and anyone else who knew West to take him seriously as a boyfriend in any event.

When I stopped having sporadic guilty feelings about the incident, I even congratulated myself. Maybe I had averted my mother's marriage to the man who would have been highly unwelcome, if not unacceptable, to the rest of the family. West was clearly too crazy to be married to anyone especially to my mother. Knowing what a snob Mother could be, even when living in the worst ghettoes, I couldn't imagine her introducing her shabby and delusional friend to her upwardly mobile sisters and their husbands. I noted that Mother never, during the time she and West "dated", ever suggested that he meet her sisters or mother.

Later that year, Mother met someone else, a maintenance man employed at Parkway and he became her boyfriend. This man, although always joking and friendly, was secretive and never let me or even Mother know too much about him or his life.(We accurately suspected he was married but didn't investigate, pursue, or share our suspicions.) He didn't come around much. He claimed he was kept too busy, when not working, to visit as he was a member of a local traveling gospel group---the Songbirds of Color. I listened to some of the records the group had produced and they had the fervent and closely harmonized sound of the Dixie Hummingbirds or the Five Blind Boys of Alabama. They traveled the "chitlin' circuit" (the segregation-generated, black entertainment network that catered to blacks) singing at black churches and nightclubs all over the South and in the larger northern cities. Lloyd had a drinking problem that had caused him to lose a kidney but Mother called herself helping him, too, as she had with West, by providing him home-cooked meals and vitamins.

I liked Lloyd. True, he wasn't handsome—--he was horse-faced--or polished. He had a shady background—--"I'm an escapee from a South Carolina chain gang. I used alligators' heads as stepping stones. They're still looking for me in South Carolina," he bragged. But, he didn't come around much, didn't stay long when he did, didn't have much to say to me or my brothers, and what he said was polite and friendly. Like West, he wasn't introduced to the family or made part of their gatherings. Occasionally, he told good, if dubiously true, stories. I loved a story he told about running out of gas in a Southern lynching town at night. He told us about finding a murdered coworker in a Parkway elevator shaft, and about a man who drank stuff like lighter fluid and turpentine, who could light his belches with a match, and whose organs eventually liquefied from his chemical imbibing. Lloyd insisted that Dr. King had schoolteacher girlfriends scattered all over the South Side. With the exception of the Dr. King story, which I refused to believe (Dr. King could do no wrong in my eyes), I delighted in these stories. Best of all, Lloyd didn't involve himself in our lives in any meaningful way. Mother, meanwhile, seemed happier and didn't give me such cold glances any more.

In the late '60's, when I was about seventeen, I accompanied a girlfriend and her family to visit their relatives in Arkansas. When we returned, and I was getting my duffle bag out of their car, Mike and Eric burst out of our building shouting, "Mr. West's dead, Mr. West's dead!"

Shocked though I was at this news, I was even more stunned to learn that West had been back on the scene for about six months and had been seeing my mother again. Apparently, although my brothers knew this and usually couldn't keep secrets, they hadn't thought to tell me. They had also forgotten they supposedly hadn't liked West any more than I did. Clearly though, my mother was definitely keeping it a secret from me.

Even with the hard heart I had kept for West, the story of his death left a bad taste in my mouth. This was how it happened. Mother, an unsuccessful and frustrated artist, had rented a small store on the far South Side of Chicago in which to sell her drawings, despite warnings from friends and family that poor blacks wouldn't or couldn't afford to buy artwork. West had been meeting her there and on the occasion of his death, my brothers were with her. As they were talking, West suddenly had a massive stroke, not only collapsing but vomiting on himself and losing control of his bowels and bladder. My brothers ran outside to summon help and asked a police officer to come assist them.

Mike was shaking as he told the story, "When the cop came back to the store, he got mad at Mr. West because he had vomited and shitted on himself. He started beating him and calling him disgusting. He told Mama Mr. West was drunk and disorderly and he was gonna have to take him to jail!"

According to Mike, instead of calling for an ambulance, the cop called for the paddy wagon and he and other officers not only roughly threw West on the back floor of the wagon but hit him a few times for good measure with their billy clubs. "Mama and I told the cop West didn't drink. He was sick and should go to a hospital. That cop just got in the squad car and pulled off."

Mother and my brothers were devastated by what they had witnessed, but also terrified, as they, too, were threatened by the cops.

West died on the way to the jail. When I spoke to my mother about the incident, she sobbed inconsolably, "Why did they do that to him? He was sick and harmless. He shouldn't have had to die. I am so sorry. I am so sorry. I'm so heartbroken," Mother kept repeating. She couldn't be comforted.

I felt bad, too, and guilty even though I had nothing to do with West's death and his horrible treatment at the hands of the cops. I was starting to recognize, if not understand, the role fate or circumstances beyond our control play in people's lives. I saw blood on my hands when I reflected on how I had split his relationship with my mother years before. After his death, some of the awkward questions and uneasy feelings that I thought I had mentally buried years ago re-emerged. *Should I not have picked that fight long ago with West? Was the "supervision" situation really as inflammatory or threatening as I believed or had I told myself this so often I had come to believe it? Wasn't my mother in the wrong for leaving me alone with West--- thus establishing, but then ignoring, a ticking bomb situation? Was it wrong for me to get rid of him in any way that I could? Was I only asking myself these questions now that I was grown or because he couldn't be a nuisance anymore? No, this wasn't about me,* I realized.

I never could answer these questions even though they circled endlessly in my mind, for months after the death and have continued to do so, intermittently, down through the years. I never again discussed his dying with Mother or my brothers. I was angry and fearful at the way the Chicago cops treated West and the fact that I knew they had done it before, got away with it, and would do it again. Ultimately, I had to acknowledge that all the pity, sorrow, guilt, anger and remorse in the world would not bring West back. He was one of those people that life always says "no" to and life had had the last word.

CHAPTER 17
GOING POSTAL

I had graduated early from high school—-I was only sixteen. I felt as if a boulder had rolled off my shoulders when I left D.P. I intended to go to college no matter how little or how much money my family had. I was accepted at the "Circle" as the University of Illinois at Chicago was then widely called, because the Congress Expressway circled around the campus. My mother sat me down and told me— "I don't have any money to send you to college. But you'll do well. You're smart. You'll figure something out." My father didn't comment on the situation at all. I knew that meant he wouldn't be aiding me financially. Mother was right because I lucked into a scholarship for the children of postal employees (like my father), financed by the Post Office, with nickels and dimes gathered from its vending machines. Still, I needed spending money and wanted job experience as well. I equated working with being an adult and was very eager to be independent financially. That spring, I passed the scheme examination-- —a test for postal employment that centered on one's ability to figure out train and mail delivery schedules. I was hired the spring before my June graduation and I started work a few days after the ceremony. Mother danced clumsily but joyfully in the living room when I got the employment news. She believed kids should get jobs as soon as they could legally do so and help out their families.

I can no longer remember what I expected-- I suppose some sort of orderly nine-to-five, kind boss and happy employee scenario. What I got was something entirely different. I was very young and naïve. The job was at the Main Post Office then referred to by black citizens as "Mayor(or Master) Daley's Plantation"—---the hulking behemoth straddling the Congress Expressway--now an empty husk abandoned for a newer building. I was assigned to the night shift in the Lock Box unit, located in the building's dank and dark basement, where clerks (also called handlers)processed junk and contest mail. As a clerk, I punched the time clock at 3:00 p.m. and spent the next eight hours sorting--—"throwing"---trays of mail. Despite the humdrum nature of throwing mail, which could have been learned by a monkey in ten minutes, there was drama enough for three jobs. This was before stories about the turbulent nature of the postal service became common and before the phrase "going postal" was coined to describe violently disgruntled and armed employees. But even then, criminal incidents occurred among workers at the job, and their fellow employees were expected to deal with them as best they could.

Immediately after I started working there, one of the female clerks came up to me and said, "Baby girl, you're young so you need to know. There's men raping women on these elevators, especially if you go up to the ninth floor cafeteria. These muthafuckin' bosses ain't gonna do nothing about it if you get caught by one of 'em neither. If you go to nine, ask one of these men around here to go with you."

That conversation sent fear racing up my spine. I silently vowed to bring my dinner with me every day so I'd never have to go up to the ninth floor cafeteria. One of my male co-workers accompanied me, standing in front of me like a bodyguard, the one time I dared to use the elevator to go up to nine. The men I worked with saw I was only sixteen and a dumb, scared, skinny sixteen at that. No one tried to take advantage of me. "Hey, 'Jail Bait'" or "'Baby Girl'" they'd call out to me when I punched in at work.

Even with the protection of my co-workers, I quickly discovered the P.O. was a place in which you had to step lightly. Some of the clerks drank the whole time they were throwing mail, openly swilling whiskey straight from the bottle. Jimmy, a good-looking clerk, would stand draining a bottle of Jack Daniels while he threw mail with one hand. Workers played sex games while on the clock. The male clerks would reach down the front of certain willing female workers' blouses and fondle their breasts or massage their butts. They didn't care whether they were seen or not. I was so young both in age and experience that I was embarrassed by the massaging and tried to look anywhere but at the partyers. I was grateful that no one seemed interested in my toothpick legs and washboard chest.

"They can see if you're stealing or going through that contest mail," an older worker told me. "They can see through that ceiling and they'll arrest your ass if they catch you." Although I had no intention of stealing or tampering with the mail, I was fascinated and puzzled by the warnings because the ceiling appeared utterly black and opaque. I couldn't tell how anyone could see through it and actually eyeball perpetrators. Still I feared that I would be seen doing something, anything, that would be considered incriminating. The supposed surveillance made me afraid even to read the back of the vacation postcards we handled. One afternoon, black-suited men showed up suddenly and clapped a male clerk in handcuffs. The Lock Box gossips claimed he had been opening contest mail and removing the money that contestants had enclosed. The watchers in the ceiling saw him do this a few times and nailed him. The legend surrounding the watchers was true after all.

There were daily fights. Some were physical and some were what we South Siders called "signifying"-- fast-paced, profane verbal battles that specially emphasized "yo mama" jokes-- obscene insults aimed at other co-workers' mothers. The fights were not just between the mail handlers themselves but between the supervisors who stood on elevated platforms, like overseers, and the workers who worked below. All the supervisors seemed to be white and all the clerks were black. I can still remember the daily, steady ricochet of nasty talk and racial slurs. Supervisor: "If you don't work harder (or come on time, or stop getting your friends to punch you in, etc.) I'm gonna write your black ass up!"

Worker: "You slimy honky M.F.! I'm gonna write up yo' ass and yo' mama's too!"

I became so used to the harsh and steady rhythm of racial slamming that it became a sort of familiar white-noise background for throwing mail. After attending my high school, I had gotten tougher about, or, at least, less sensitive to racial slurs. However, witnessing the sexual shenanigans that were going on embarrassed me no end. But no matter how foul or crude the verbal fights got, I either tuned them out or cracked up at the trash-talking.

The P.O. was one of the few places that would hire people who had recently been released from mental hospitals. One of the recently released was a clerk who never spoke to nor looked at anyone. He steadily threw mail and hawked loudly and spat wetly in a tin can every three minutes or so, to everyone's disgust. One of the male handlers, a burly, no-nonsense guy, said, "I'ma put a stop to this shit. This is so goddamn nasty." We all gathered around to see him stop the hawker in his tracks. When the burly guy approached him, the hawker jumped up, jammed his hand in his pocket and gripped something shaped like a gun. He stared slowly, coldly and emotionlessly at each of us in turn. One of the women said backing off, "He **is** crazy, y'all. I don't wanna see him use that on nobody." When he looked especially hard at the burly guy, Burly quickly leaped behind a packaging machine. No one complained or interfered with the throat clearing and hawking after that.

Other incidents happened. Once while throwing mail on "the line", as the mail rows were called, I looked up and caught the eye of another female worker-- a hostile, hard looking sister, with a shellacked "freeze" hairdo—"What the fuck are you looking at you little bitch," she whispered. "I'm gonna kick yo' ass if you look this way again."

She didn't have to tell me twice. I kept my eyes down, while quaking in my boots, for the next two weeks but, to my relief, that worker never appeared on my line again.

A particular incident, one lazy summer afternoon, sticks in my memory the most. While there were fights aplenty at the P.O., over everything and nothing, this fight broke out between two sixty-something women who both looked like grannies straight out of church. One even wore an apron to work every day. Both were gray-haired, fat and wore bifocals and orthopedic shoes. The fight started because the two disagreed about whether a big, grime-encrusted window in the corner of the work space should be open or shut since there was no air conditioning and few fans. I heard a raspy, "Keep that window open bitch or I'll have to cut you" coming from their direction. As I and others drew closer to see what was happening, the disagreement suddenly escalated into a full-fledged fight. The two elderly women simultaneously pulled switchblades and, squatting, circled each other like sumo wrestlers. The other workers formed an excited ring around them, some urging on their favorite fighter. "Go, baby! Cut that bitch!" one of the more avid employees shouted.

I was so shocked and nervous I ran behind the crowd and peeked around some of the folks standing ringside. Oh, My God. I was about to see my first up-close murder and no one was rushing to stop it. The battling grannies swiped and stabbed at each other viciously, although neither landed a blade, until someone yelled for a boss to break it up. Once the fight was stopped, the two were not ejected from the floor but went back to calmly throwing mail--just another day at the P.O. I was aghast. The old women I knew, like my grandmother, did nothing but talk about their illnesses and exchange potting recipes for their geraniums and petunias. Their disagreements were over who made the best coconut layer cake and their fighting was done with dust mops.

The next time I saw my father, who worked at the same facility occasionally, I told him about the fight and my fear the two women would murder each other. He shrugged and said flatly, "Well, Baby, that's life at the Post Office. This is what you get when you let a lot of crazy niggers work for you. Just stay out of their way." My father never thought there was anything wrong with the Post Office or, if there was, you just avoided the troublemakers. I didn't bring it up again. I was leaving the P.O. for college and putting this loony stuff behind me.

To be fair, there were good times as well and the other workers were always kind to me. And, despite the raw and loose atmosphere at the P.O., the mail always got where it was supposed to go-—on time. Every Friday, someone would wheel a gurney of fried chicken, potato salad and scotch into the Lock Box. Workers would turn on their transistors, and I can still remember Bobby Hebb singing *Sunny* as we ate wings while I sipped Coke and the others hit the whiskey. I was glad when the college semester began but also grateful that I had experienced an adult or at least adult-rated workplace. I never returned to work at the Post Office again, even though my father, always in survival mode and about holding onto a steady job, periodically urged me to: "It's a great job, Baby! We got a strong union and a guaranteed pension! Forget those niggers you used to work with in the Lock Box and keep your head down. You'll do all right!"

CHAPTER 18
COLLEGE AND DR. KING

"Clear this street in the name of the state of Illinois", the cop with a face like a raw steak yelled at us, as he squinted against the cold wind.

That April morning in 1968, my friends, Karen, Suzanne and I braced ourselves against the wind and each other, locked hands and kneeled gingerly, across from the bleak caves and smoky-windowed towers of the new campus of the University of Illinois at Chicago, on freezing, dirty Halsted Street. I felt glass and metallic grit cut into my knees.

The evening before, I had received a telephone call. I could hardly recognize my friend Suzanne's voice it was so choked: "Kim, someone assassinated Dr. King! Girl, what are we gonna do?" While I had heard and read as had everyone else that Dr. King was continually threatened, he always seemed to keep on going and fighting for us blacks. I had hoped the threats were just racist smoke-blowing from southern whites. When he gave his "mountaintop speech" during the March on Washington, I thought he was just being grandly oratorical when he said "I may not get there with you."

Suzanne's news hit me like a punch in the stomach. I collapsed backward on the raggedy couch in our kitchen. I couldn't breathe. "What happened Suzy?" I asked. "I didn't hear about this at all," I cried. I kept repeating that as if my not hearing it would change things. I couldn't stop panting. My lungs and throat felt dry and burned as if I'd been running. "He was somewhere down south, Memphis or somewhere, and someone just shot him down on his motel balcony. I don't know all the facts. Mama is watching TV to see what happened," Suzanne said.

What were we going to do, indeed? I was too stunned to cry. My shock was quickly turning to fear. "Will these whites try to kill us all?" I asked. "Where are the other leaders--Dr. Abernathy and them? What are they saying happened?" "What do they want us to do?"

"I don't think they know anything either," she said wearily. "Supposedly, Jesse Jackson was there when he got shot and is going to talk on TV tonight about it." Suzanne and I talked off and on until about 11:30, late for me. Our conversation circled as we hashed over and over the same bits of information we already knew or the updates her mother shouted at us from their couch in front of the TV. We kept asking each other, "Will we all be next?" What would this mean?

When my mother came home from work, she glumly grabbed some cheap steaks and slapped them on the broiler. She had heard the news at work. I don't know where my brothers were. For once, my stomach was churning too much to eat. When Mother finished eating, she started playing solitaire——a sure and familiar sign she was upset and trying to marshal her mind and emotions. Her mouth was turned down, her voice was weak. All she would say is, "White folks won't let us have nothing, especially someone fighting for us colored folks." Neither she nor I cried nor did we turn on TV. You can be too depressed, too sad, too scared, to cry. The next morning, I felt dizzy and high as I had slept poorly. I was still nauseous and headachy. My mother, who had given up on teaching and was now a caseworker for the Illinois Department of Welfare, had thrown on her one dress, and gone to work --she never missed a day. I suddenly decided to get dressed for school. After all, what good would staying at home do?

I met Suzanne and Karen at the door to the Student Union. Standing at the door of the Union, arms crossed and frowning were two guys, Joe Lampkin and Travis Crandall, joined-at-the-hip, self-nominated leaders of the sketchy campus black militant group, the Black Students' Organization. They led mostly because they hollered "black power" and "revolution" louder and pounded tables harder and more often than the rest of us. They stood there and ordered every black student who entered to go to the Illinois Room and await further instructions.

We filed into the already crammed Illinois Room-- a small auditorium-- with the other black students who came to school that day. Joe and Travis ran up on the stage.

Travis thundered his complaint to the crowd, "This morning, them goddamn honkies in the University president's office told me us blacks couldn't hold a memorial service for Dr. King in this room. Can y'all believe that shit?"

"They kill him and then try to stop us from mourning his loss as a people!" Joe yelled. "Travis and I are going out right now and kneel on Halsted Street and keep these honkies from going to their damn jobs!" "They'll know that we ain't fuckin' around with their asses. We want y'all to join us. Dr. King would want us to do this."

One girl in the front row timidly asked, "What should we do if we're arrested?" Travis hollered, "Go to jail with your head up high, sister! That's what you do! He repeated, "Dr. King would want us to do this."

I stood with the other black students listening to the two's fiery speeches that morning. I was numbed and befuddled by the sudden assassination and hesitant about their heated demand that we go out immediately to the street. It flashed through my mind: *Neither Joe nor Travis are giving us instructions about what we should do while or after we kneel out there or exactly what this protest will accomplish. Our going out there isn't going to raise Dr. King from the dead. Will it really mean anything?* I squelched those thoughts with quick guilt. I remembered seeing photographs of Dr. King marching in Chicago's Marquette Park and recognizing one of my old white boy classmates from high school as he lobbed a brick at King's head. I remembered older pictures of Dr. King marching on Washington, marching in Selma, Alabama, leading the bus boycott in Montgomery, Alabama, writing letters from jail, imploring America to be better, to honor and respect all its citizens. He fought so we could vote, sit at the front of a bus, sit down at restaurant, have some dignity. Maybe just kneeling in and of itself would show some courage or resistance, some anger, to what we called "the white power structure" about Dr. King's tragic death.

On the other hand, I was uncertain. I had never been part of a formal or informal protest. I was in my second year of undergraduate work but already deep into plans for law school. I had a double major-——English and political science--and I spent a lot of time studying and trying to get grades that would get me into a good law school and away from my family. In a past moment of what I deemed clarity, I had decided my law school dream and visions of future happiness lay in escaping my always-broke, depressing family and our stagnant relationships.

I had a new health fear that added to my desire to flee Chicago and home. When I was nineteen, I had discovered a lump in my breast as hard and rounded as a medium-sized marble. I was terrified, but because our family had no health insurance, no doctor would treat the lump other than to vaguely assure me it was probably benign. "You're young—it's probably nothing," two of them said. I tried to tell myself they were right and not think about what it could mean. My hope, though, was that if I could leave Chicago for law school, some doctor somewhere would take this lump out and I'd live happily ever after.

Uncertain health and dysfunctional family aside, I was obsessed with having an absolutely clean record to begin my future "happy" life. A clean record meant no trouble with the law, no babies before marriage, not even a lot of dates because they could pose a distraction. I had tunnel vision where my yet-to-come career was concerned. Some of my older relatives, including my mother, had gone to college. The family had produced educators but no other professionals. My dream was to become the first lawyer. I'd long held this dream and had been encouraged by family because I was studious and argumentative.

Jet, Ebony, and Establishment newspapers as well as the black folks' "grapevine" carried stories about arrests, imprisonment, physical attacks, and the financial and academic ruin of student protestors. Those stories had made a deep impression on me. If I was arrested as a protestor, would that be the end of all my plans? I can still hear my mother's voice telling me that I was always too self-absorbed. This criticism made me feel raw and exposed as a selfish person but it didn't change my behavior much. Today when I reflect on those days, I prefer to believe that I was not selfish-—just young, cautious, determined, and terrified of violence.

So here we were, being ordered by Travis and Joe to get out there and stop traffic to honor or avenge Dr. King, who was freshly dead at the hand of unknown racist assassins. My thoughts raced and tangled: I was afraid of Chicago's notorious brutal, Negro-hating cops but Dr. King had faced down southern and northern cops, snarling dogs, water hoses, jail and death to free us from discrimination. I didn't want to chance arrest but Dr. King had gone to jail many times in the name of freedom for people like me.

Suddenly, I decided I was overthinking the whole matter and that I should be part of some organized reaction to Dr. King's slaying no matter the consequences. So I followed Joe and Travis to the street that day although I'll admit I was wary of them both. They were good looking dudes, maybe too much so, sporting huge atom bomb afros, bushy moustaches (full, dead nineteenth century president sideburns.) They wore shades indoors and outdoors, winter and summer, and always wore cool-looking army fatigues or leather jackets like the Black Panthers'. They made full use of their looks and always seemed to have gorgeous female students hanging around them. I was not interested in being part of their "poontang posse," and always assumed Travis and Joe were using them as groupies and foot soldiers for their activism. One day, I had overheard Travis admonish his little troupe of followers to reject cute white guys, "Sisters--love your black brothers don't reject them. Y'all should be digging the witch doctor, not Tarzan."

Travis and Joe also seemed sneaky to me. Their track record as head militants wasn't good. A couple of months earlier, there had been an impromptu rally of black students called by a firebrand sister, Lydia, because she found the two had embezzled some dues-generated funds from the Black Students' Organization. It seems that under the guise of meeting with other black student leaders in North Carolina, Joe and Travis had gone down there and spent the whole time shacked up at a no-tell motel with (gasp!) white women.

My girlfriends and I had attended that rally full of indignation, more because of the white girl hook-up, which, in our view, was the worst thing a black guy could do in those days, than the stolen funds. After all, the money stolen was all of about $500.00, but there were few black men on campus available to be our boyfriends. Most had been drafted or were struggling to make good grades and stay out of the army. It was the principle of the thing, as we told each other. The highlight of the rally for me had been the South Side tongue-lashing Linda gave the two: "Y'all are not leaders. Y'all are thieves. Y'all couldn't lead me to water even if I was thirsty. You couldn't lead me to food even if I wanted to eat!" The two squirmed at the scolding but she was unable to get them to return the money. Nevertheless, as my friend Karen said, "At least she got them dogs told!"

So, although I distrusted the leadership of Joe and Travis, this wasn't one of their usual and frequent rallies in the school's lounges decrying generic racism. Their rallying cry this time was about an event, a murder so horrible, so total in effect, so earth-shaking that we all had a duty to do something drastic about it, to show some outrage. Didn't we? Surely, this was not the usual Joe and Travis drama but about trying to say something significant. We all had to put aside our petty fears and concerns and show the world we wouldn't stand still for this monumental grievance, this evil.

    I don't know what was going through my friends' minds or why they were willing to follow Joe and Travis to the street. We didn't have time to discuss the call to protest. But my friends and I, as well as many other students, trailed behind a fist-shaking Joe and Travis out to Halsted. Halsted was lined with shouting crowds of white and black students, but I was so scared and the shouts so loud, I couldn't hear clearly or understand what they were saying. I took a deep breath to steady myself, linked arms with my friends and we all knelt on the filthy street. As we were stooping, cop cars screeched up Halsted toward us from every direction. Several of the cars had fenced-in rears jammed with K-9 corps dogs that were already foaming at the mouth and snapping at the windows. At the sight of the dogs and the bellowing cops waving guns and clubs my heart bounced up and down between my throat and stomach like a yo-yo.

    And then suddenly we saw them—-Joe and Travis. We had lost track of them while we were marching down to the street. They were across the street from us, together, backing away from the curb and tiptoeing away into the crowd. Suzanne hollered, "Look y'all! Joe and Travis! They're getting away!"

    I was shocked and angry. Those two guys weren't going to join us in this protest about the death of Dr. King after they had urged, no ordered, us to get out there. They had made us feel guilty for hesitating, for fearing the consequences of a sit-in. As one, my friends and I jumped to our feet, then hopped backward and up on the curb. We weren't going to go to jail if our so-called leaders weren't willing to put their necks on the line. As I backed away, I thought, nervously: *There has to be another way to honor King rather than having a dog chew on my ass, especially when those fake leaders are watching safely from the sidelines while it's happening.*

My friends and I marched right back into the Student Union, fussing about Joe and Travis all the way. We grimly agreed they were no good, that we had been mightily betrayed. Suzanne grumbled, "We should have known Travis and Joe weren't for real. It ain't like they haven't pulled this type of shit before! I'm just mad we followed behind them like little dogs. Those fools!"

I threw in furiously, "Those trifling Negroes! They actually wanted to see us get arrested!"

Yes, I seethed with the others about the treachery of Joe and Travis but secretly felt I had dodged a bullet. *What would have happened if they hadn't flaked out on us and we'd gone ahead with our half-baked plan to protest the murder of Dr. King by kneeling on Halsted?*

While we were fuming, we started hearing rumors from the other students that blacks had begun rioting on the West Side of Chicago not far from where the school was located. My anger faded into stark fear at what was happening-—events seemed to be snowballing. My group of friends talked quickly about what might happen if we were caught in a riot: violence, arrests, strandings on the West Side, inability to buy food, reach transportation or get home to our families. The scary possibilities were endless. In just a few hours, we had zoomed from the aborted protest to possibly being caught in a full-fledged riot.

After talking together about what could happen, we decided to walk together downtown, rather than take the el, and buy food at the Stop and Shop grocery store in case we had to hole up at our homes and were unable to shop for necessary provisions. I have no idea why we thought it was up to us to bring food home to our South Side families, as our homes already had food. None of us had ever been responsible for feeding our families, but that day this became foremost on our minds. I don't know what we thought we were accomplishing or demonstrating by walking downtown. Perhaps we thought we were displaying some sort of bravery, but I'm not sure. We walked, or rather marched, to the Loop, chanting "Umgawa, umgawa, you know we got black power! "Power to the people!" And, "You've killed the dreamer not the dream!" As we marched, the streets were almost deserted and unnaturally quiet, so quiet we could hear the tramp of our feet, hear glass breaking, see smoke rising to our west, hear fire engines screaming. I could smell the musk of old wood and plaster overlaid with smoke. Then the quiet broke completely and we heard the distant shouts of angry West Siders and felt the rumbling vibration under our feet of crashing buildings going up in flames.

At that time, the neighborhoods west of the Loop, were mainly a mixture of black, Italian and some Latino families. Even closer to the Loop was the infamous Madison Street Skid Row area, where homeless men lay by the dozens in front of rescue missions and boarded-up shops. As we marched through those areas, we saw people milling on the sidewalks almost as if in a daze. One woman standing on the sidewalk shouted out to us: "Sisters, Mayor Daley done gone on the tv and radio and told the cops to shoot to kill us all. Y'all better get on home!" We walked faster. Her warning terrified me so much I fantasized that I felt one of those bullets tearing into my back. When we reached the Loop, we ran into the Stop and Shop, threw canned goods into a few shopping carts, got the stuff bagged and paid for and jumped on the bus home. Despite the increasingly jittery situation in the city and the sounds of the approaching riot, the Jeffery and South Park buses were still going out to the southeast side where we lived.

Now, some forty years later, I get together at least once annually with some of the women I went with to the Circle. The subject of that long ago "protest" always comes up. We rehash the betrayal and our indignation at that time, although with some laughs at the slimy way Joe and Travis escaped from the Halsted wanna-be confrontation. What surprises me is that I am the only one to cop to the cowardice crown although I realize perhaps I was the only coward. I am happy to confess I was glad the protest was a bust, although Joe and Travis certainly should have been boiled in oil. After all, we later found out some students who they had urged into the street had been arrested at that protest. After that, perhaps motivated by guilt over their cowardice, Joe and Travis kept a low profile, weren't seen on campus much and never tried to "lead" any more protests.

CHAPTER 19
82ND AND CHAPPELL

At the end of my freshman year in college, my family had moved to the South Shore neighborhood on 82nd and Chappell. This was our first genuine upper-middle class neighborhood, and the small, one and a half story bungalow was our first detached single-family home. We had loved the apartment on Minerva, despite the rodents and conflict with our neighbors. Until about a year before we moved from there, in 1967, that neighborhood had been quiet and untroubled. Then trouble had started to mount. The co-op residents had never liked us or renters in general. They were angry that Mrs. Cates had sublet her apartment to a single mother with three kids, including two roughhousing boys. They complained to Mother and then Mrs. Cates about the noise and our loud footsteps on their ceiling. Then "Colonel" (we found out he really wasn't one) Crawford in our building blew his own head off one night and his sour-faced widow started picking on us in earnest. Kitty was the main issue. This building had developed a serious rodent problem like some of our previous homes. We could hear them racing around in the walls all night. Kitty had caught and killed quite a few. As far as I was concerned, she was doing the whole building a favor after the "high-toned" residents had just ignored the growing problem. Mrs. Crawford made a big stink about Kitty, though, calling Mrs. Cates and claiming we had "overrun the building with pets" and had brought the mouse problem to the building ourselves. Mother and I had several unpleasant shouting matches with Mrs. Crawford about Kitty, but we ultimately lost because the other co-op owners sided with her and, after all, we were only renters. Mrs. Cates suddenly decided she had heard enough complaints, wanted her apartment back and was going to return from Ohio.

Then there was the gang factor. When we were on Minerva, young men would gather under the lamppost near my window (although Mrs. Crawford routinely called the police on them) and sing doo-wop songs like the Platter's *Great Pretender*. Now, the type of young guys hanging around corners had changed drastically. The Blackstone and P-stone Rangers had become a sudden threatening phenomenon. When my oldest brother Mike started junior high in the area, he was robbed and beaten almost every day. Gang members stood around in "gouster" uniform (fedoras, doo-rags and wifebeaters with baggy trousers) eyeing everyone. Boys were so endangered in East Woodlawn (they had to join the gang or die) that Mother decided we had to get out. There were a lot of mysterious fires that were said to be set by the gangs. The rumors were that Mayor Daley got the gangs to burn unwanted people (blacks) out so the University of Chicago professors could move back in, reclaim the spacious buildings, and re-gentrify the area. Mother dashed around looking for a place to buy this time, and found a small, neat, two-bedroom bungalow on 82nd and Chappell in the South Shore neighborhood. She pulled together $13,000, all her savings, and bought it.

It was 1967 and South Shore was the nicest area we had ever lived in. There were blocks of sterling small brown and blonde brick bungalows punctuated with immaculate two-story flats. Each bungalow had stained or art glass side windows and when walking the blocks, it was like looking at a row of earringed houses. Their small but identical green lawns looked like a never-ending emerald necklace. Many of the blacks who had moved to South Shore were professionals, and in its northern section, around East End Avenue, there were actual mansions. When we moved to Chappell, our block still had white residents although, within the next year, one by one they moved away. Our next-door neighbors, the Jenkins, were the last whites on the block. When we first moved in, the tall, skinny, husband went out of his way to tell Mother and me that he and his wife "weren't running away from their home because the block was integrating." That made us feel a little less like pariahs until one night a few months later, I got up to get some water and saw the Jenkins throwing their stuff in the back of a moving van. I opened the door and the husband shouted out to me as he was revving up the truck: "Family emergency! We've got to move to Kentucky!"

Around this time, our home life became more troubled. Mike suddenly declared himself to be not merely militant but a revolutionary. "We're going to off these pigs!" he'd shout as he paced around our house dressed in black. "Black people need to organize for an armed overthrow of this government!" Recently, Mike had threatened to join the Black Panthers or some secret, nameless "revolutionary" organization that only he and a mysterious friend named Mr. K seemed to know about. My mother was frightened. "Kim, you've got talk to him. I've argued and argued, but he won't listen. Some white man is going to kill him if he keeps this up!" The Black Panthers Fred Hampton and Mark Clark had recently been killed in their beds by the Chicago police. Scared and angry black college students and their parents believed it to be a planned assassination and a warning to other blacks who might be thinking about joining that organization. I knew that was what Mother feared.

I myself thought Mike was all talk. He was never in the streets actually doing any of the things he threatened, and I remembered the scared little boy who needed Eric and me to protect him from neighborhood bullies. But I understood why my mother feared for him----many black youths had been shot and killed in the persistent racial turmoil that had affected the nation and our city. She just didn't want him to be a statistic.

I cornered him one day. "Hey, Mike," I said, "stop scaring Mother with all this Black Panther talk. She doesn't want to see your black ass end up like Fred Hampton and them. Have you forgotten what happened to Mr. West? He wasn't harming anybody and they killed him."

He blinked rapidly as he did when he was mad or challenged about something he'd done or said. "You all are toms! You just don't want to see black men defending the black community!" he shouted.

"Look, fool!," I replied, we don't disagree with you that we are living like colonists and third class citizens, but we don't want to see you end up in a casket. You ain't Stokely Carmichael. I want you to stop talking this shit around Mother, and that includes claiming you and Mr. K and those other undercover clowns are going to war with the cops. Let's have some peace in this house for once."

Despite our talk, Mike really never stopped his inflammatory talk about armed insurrections, but it never translated into action. He never joined any of the more militant organizations, to my mother's relief. However, since he was jobless and always in the house, we were still inundated by his continued focus on and bluster about race and what he considered to be justified and inevitable retaliatory violence from the black community. While he ranted on, he would drive us crazy by playing all day at top volume, the thundering sound of the band *Chicago's* latest album.

There were other problems in our little paradise. My sharp-tongued, energetic grandmother lived with us full time, but her diabetes had caused a sad, serious physical and mental decline. Her eyesight and hearing were almost gone and her dementia was total----she didn't recognize us anymore. Mother had to hire a helper to watch, clean and feed her during the day.

Making all this worse was Mother's insistence on allowing a non-paying, larcenous, teenage boarder, Edward, to stay in our attic. Edward was a high school buddy of Mike's. Mike had told Mother that Edward's supposedly cruel parents had inexplicably kicked him out, leaving him nowhere to go. Mother's tradition of helping castaway males emerged in full force and she invited Edward to move in. The fact that our jewelry and kitchen appliances started disappearing, after Ed moved in, didn't faze her. The fact that Mike and he were no longer pals and that none of us liked or trusted him didn't either. Nor did the fact that he made the little house seem crowded. We had only two small bedrooms and a tiny unheated sewing room. Mother and I slept in one. Grandma, Mike and Eric slept in the other two. But this did not change her mind. Our house had seemed spacious and private when we had moved in. Now it seemed packed, noisy, uncomfortable and, in some way, no longer our home. All these conflicting emotions and personalities resulted in a rising bitterness that kept our house in a tense and anxious state. I longed to escape the house, my family and Chicago itself even more. I had had enough.

CHAPTER 20
CRAZY COLLEGE JOBS

During my sophomore year of college, one of my friends helped me get a work-study job in a day camp situated in an abandoned Catholic church on the near West Side. The church had once had a Polish or Irish congregation which had moved away when the neighbors got darker. A white upperclassman, Rick Powers, started the day camp with some type of governmental funding, and we helped children in the primary grades with their reading and math and played games with them for a few hours a day. I didn't make much money but I had the Post Office scholarship and lived at home so I didn't care. The kids were fun and we held dancing contests so the little boys could show us who could dance the most like James Brown. But things started going downhill. One of the white student volunteers was robbed and blurted at me, "You people are always stealing things!" on his angry way out. He discouraged other potential volunteers by telling them we were working with a bunch of black thieves. The church had huge rats, one of which tried to come in the playroom, walking like a man on its hind legs. We threw pop bottles and cans at him but he was so bold it was tough to drive him off. I had an overwhelming fear of rats and rodents in general and had to force myself to come to work after that. At the end of my junior year, the City of Chicago announced it was going to demolish the church and other abandoned buildings in the area to discourage crime and vandalism. Powers told me, "The Catholic Church told the City to go ahead and tear it down. They didn't care."

We closed the day camp and I got a job as a gofer in the career office at the University administration building. No one came in that office and I can't remember anyone getting a job through our efforts. We just stood around all day yakking. Cindy, one of our office managers, jumped up on a desk one day, whipped off her coke-bottle glasses and announced she was gay. This was a stunning and brave announcement for 1969, even on a college campus. The other office manager was one of a kind: a very young but efficient Mennonite from rural Indiana wearing traditional Mennonite garb--- white bonnet, long black dress with apron, wire-rimmed glasses, sturdy shoes. Her name was Hannah and she was very religious but surprisingly lived with a black guy in the infamous Robert Taylor Homes project. No one knew how she ended up in Chicago and with a black boyfriend to boot. Hannah was kind to me, as she was to everyone, but when she overheard me mouthing off to someone about "white women taking our men"(I didn't have a boyfriend and blamed everyone but myself for that), she spontaneously invited me to dinner at the Taylor Homes. "I'm going to prove to you there can be love between the races," she said.

I was scared shitless at the thought of going anywhere near those projects, which I had read and heard were the most notoriously crime-ridden in the nation, but I was curious. I wanted to get a look at the black boyfriend and see how Hannah was living. Lloyd, Mother's boyfriend, dropped me off and picked me up after the dinner. I heard him bark a laugh as I glanced around fearfully and scurried into the building. I was sure I could be shot any minute. I climbed on the pissy-smelling elevator, its walls marked with gang scrawlings.

Hannah was dressed in her traditional garments. The apartment was much like Parkway's standard units: metal door, small, boxy rooms, tiny windows, miniscule kitchen, loud R&B blasting through the hall, odors of cooking and urine. It was neatly and sparsely furnished, the boyfriend quiet and pleasant. I was polite. They were quietly affectionate with each other and I could see the love between them. The dinner was peas, some sort of broiled meat and chocolate pudding. We could have been eating in LaGrange. It went well but didn't answer my unasked questions. How had they ended up together in the most dangerous project in the nation and why did they stay?

CHAPTER 21
GRADUATION AND CASEWORKING

When I graduated from college in 1970 at twenty, I wanted to go to law school right away. Going to law school was what I regarded as step one of my plan for permanent escape from my family. I emphatically refused even to apply at a local law school despite my father's astonishing request that I go to the University of Chicago "to be close to my mother". I was elated when I was accepted at the University of Michigan's law school. But my measly bank account wouldn't supplement my small tuition-only scholarship nor help with room and board. My parents had no money to give me so I needed money and I needed it fast.

I had been working the summer after graduation as a credentials analyst for the University of Illinois reviewing the transcripts of college applicants and deciding who would be admitted. The job was underpaid and monotonous, so my mother, who had been a Chicago caseworker for about four years, urged me to apply for a job at the Illinois Department of Welfare. My mother was neutral towards her job. She didn't seem to like it much, but neither did she complain about it. She was friendly with most of her co-workers and, as a single mother, had expressed sympathetic concern to me for the struggling single mothers in her caseload. I took and passed the Illinois Department of Welfare's Caseworker I exam. The caseworker job paid $7,000 a year--a clear improvement over the $5,000 annual salary I was making turning down college applicants. My mother was even happier than she had been with my Post Office and college-tutoring jobs. She often explained to me and my brothers that she believed every adult child should have a job, be self-supporting and ready to contribute money to the family if necessary. A job was everything. She did acknowledge that all jobs were flawed in some way--—that was life--but she thought kids should tough it out. She gave me no indication that casework would be risky or overly bureaucratic in any way. I was so overjoyed to get a better job that I didn't ask about any potential drawbacks or challenges.

I was trained for about a week with other successful applicants in downtown Chicago at headquarters. The training focused solely on the reams of paperwork to be done and regulations to be mastered. The training supervisor at my assigned office on the South Side wasn't very specific about the actual work either. She told me, "Just do the job--go in the field, and make sure the clients are eating, can pay their rent and utilities and know where the clinics are. You'll catch on."

The office was located in a dingy, two-story walkup building. I sat with about fifty other staffers in a large, open dirty- beige-painted room as brightly lit as an operating theater. There were two always-scowling female supervisors, one a dark, heavy-set ex-Marine (we called her Tank) and the other a yellow, stiff-haired, angular person(we called her Broomstick)who endlessly circled the room like sharks. Tunnel-black eyes darting around like flies on shit, the ex-Marine pointed and hollered "Get to work, you!" at those caseworkers who appeared to be slacking. I started hunching down in my seat almost immediately after I started working there so they wouldn't notice me. Thank God, it worked.

The break room became my refuge. Tank and Broom never joined us there. I didn't work closely with most of the habitués of the break room but one has stuck in my mind because she was so funny. Loud, overweight, toothless, badly dyed flame haired Mrs. Mink dominated the break room with a crude but hilarious running commentary on her life. She lounged on break in the stretched out orange dress she always wore, meaty arms propped on the back of the shabby break room couch. She bragged and joked incessantly about everything. One favorite story from her was how much the fried chicken and mashed potatoes, no-gravy, dinners she and her husband enjoyed made them fart. "I told my husband, ooh, honey, I don't know who's worse you or me! What did that chicken eat anyhow?" she'd say, laughing, and we laughed, too---—at and with her.

Once when she told this story, this story, one of the women in my unit whispered, "I wonder if her husband is farting when he's rapping to the young girls at those lounges he hangs out at." She was referring to Mr. Mink's reputation as a partier and player.

When she did work at her desk Mrs. Mink had almost daily public cussing battles with the training supervisor, another hulking redheaded female. Each claimed to live in the ritziest neighborhood--—although they both lived in the same segregated, working-class neighborhoods we all lived in--and drove the newest Cadillac. Sometime during the day, we'd hear a loud "Go to hell, you fat bitch!", from one or the other (we laughed at this since they both topped 300 pounds) or, "I'm gonna beat your ass!" Although Tank was always on the watch for loafers, she said nothing to these two. Perhaps she thought they would curse her out publicly, too. The other caseworkers ignored these mock battles and after a while I did too. Surprisingly, they lightened the somewhat grim atmosphere a bit.

The office was divided into units. I was assigned to a unit headed by a Mrs. Hadley, a good looking, sixty-ish woman with velvety camel-colored skin and glorious, snowy white hair. She wore a double set of goose egg-sized diamond wedding rings although I heard her husband had deserted her decades before.

Hadley was a weasel and thoroughly disliked by the workers in our unit. I hadn't been there long before I learned that she regularly tattled to Tank and Broomstick about supposed office rule-infractions by her subordinates. She spent most of her time creeping from desk to desk fretting that we not anger "them" (the nameless, faceless bosses in downtown Chicago) and that we do everything "they" told us to. Besides Hadley, the unit consisted of a senior caseworker named Gayle, a slender, intelligent Black Muslim woman, and a stocky sister, Charlie, who was rumored to have had a baby by a recipient or a recipient's man. The final unit member was a thin, utterly serious white woman, Kate, from Wisconsin. Kate talked ceaselessly and proudly about her membership in the Communist Party and her avid feminist and Vietnam war protest activities.

The job was both monotonous and potentially dangerous. Richard Nixon, our then president, was considered, at least by us blacks, to be unsympathetic to the plight and economic problems of the poor. The economy was in recession. Nixon had expanded the endless and unpopular Vietnamese War into Cambodia. The Biafran war was ongoing and African babies were starving. The Chicago Seven were on trial. Students had been mowed down at Kent State and Jackson State universities. It had been a mere two years since Dr. King and Robert Kennedy were assassinated and only seven since President Kennedy was killed. There was a constant air of violence and economic and physical unrest in America. We had hazardous jobs with a volatile recipient population and often were in the position of denying money to desperate people. The fact that the sums involved were small and we were only employees doing our jobs didn't lessen their anger. All of us had observed that fury seething under the surface of our relations with the clients.

I wrote summaries of my visits to recipients, talked with recipients by phone (usually about their frequent relocations because of fires or stolen checks), and calculated the amounts due each recipient. For the remainder of a typical week, I visited the recipients at their homes, which was termed "going out in the field." Before going out in the field, we were forced to sit in weekly meetings to receive leaden instructions for caseworkers from "them," relayed through Hadley. She gave fluttery little speeches conveying our marching orders. "Ladies, this is required. You must check the recipients' bathrooms to see if the boyfriends or children's daddies are hiding in there. If you don't see them in the bathrooms, you must then check the bedrooms. Also check to see if the fathers are actually living there as that is prohibited. Please do not let the mothers see you checking. 'They' (the bosses) will be extremely angry if they find you case workers are not checking for this vital information."

The lectures aside, I looked forward to the field days, because they gave me a sense of freedom---even in an iffy neighborhood. I could also wear jeans, which were forbidden in the office. Wearing jeans helped when I had to run away from aggressive men and dangerous stray dogs. Along with my fluffy Afro, the jeans made me look as if I belonged in the neighborhood.

Hadley had assigned me to the Grand Crossing District---the southeastern edge of Englewood, a decaying neighborhood primarily composed of single mothers and kids who lived in dilapidated, wood-frame houses, loitering men and dogs. I usually walked around my district to meet with my clients, mostly mothers receiving aid to dependent children(ADC), and then I walked home to South Shore down South Chicago Avenue. That street was an ugly slash running southeast to the steel mills and Mexican neighborhoods. I'd walk down South Chicago with its block after block of eerily silent junkyards and filthy-windowed and abandoned small factories. These were broken up occasionally by teetering, ancient but occupied two-story flat buildings.

In those days, a welfare mother was not supposed to be living with the presumed father of the children if he was unable or unwilling to support them and the children. The mothers were prohibited from living with any man, for that matter. If a man was found in the home, the mother could be cut off welfare. For caseworkers, spying on the mothers could be dangerous. Any adverse assumptions or decisions we made about men we thought we saw in someone's home could mean the difference between eating or not eating to those women and their children. Since we had to call to arrange the visits, by the time we got there most of the smarter boyfriends or husbands were gone--if they existed at all. But, sooner or later, some caseworkers encountered boyfriends or recipients who were belligerent about the not-so-subtle checking and peeking around washrooms and bedrooms. When I first began, Gayle told me that Charlie had been pursued and punched by two men after a visit. There was also speculation by some caseworkers that Charlie's baby might have been the result of a rape. No one was sure and Charlie wouldn't say. The supervisors apparently hadn't bothered to investigate.

I was an unwilling and incompetent spy. I believed these women were wrongly forbidden to have male companionship simply because they were poor and black. Their love lives were none of my business. However, at the end of every visit, I would ask the mother if I could use her bathroom. I'd close the door, stand there for about two minutes, flush the toilet and leave the home immediately. I didn't ever look in bedrooms unless they were visible from the room where the client and I sat. Even then, I peeked quickly and perfunctorily. That way, I did as I was ordered, but on my own terms. My quick peeks never revealed men. If the recipients noticed me peeking, they pretended not to. Less perilous physically although more mentally torturous was our duty to ask recipients questions from what we called "the "list." These questions were supposedly designed to ferret out information about the putative fatherhood of specific children and to determine the fathers' whereabouts and willingness and ability to pay child support. The questions went like this: "Where did your intercourse take place—home, hotel, or motel? How many times did intercourse occur on each occasion? Did the intercourse take place during the day or at night? How long did the intercourse take on each occasion? Please provide the name or names of your partner(s) during each intercourse described above. Are you still in a relationship with the partner(s) of each intercourse event? If not, please provide an explanation for the break-up or termination of the above-described relationship. Please provide the names of other males or partners who might be the father of your dependent children."

There was nothing I hated so much as asking these questions, both because I was uncomfortable asking sexual questions of anyone and because I didn't believe the information was my or the state's business. Nor did I believe asking these particular questions resulted in finding the fathers and making them pay. During the year I was a caseworker, no deadbeat dads, to my knowledge, were brought to heel. This ineffectiveness might have been because caseworkers only halfheartedly asked the demeaning questions or because the mothers weren't foolish enough to give up information that would affect their financial survival.

The somewhat technical jargon we used was often perplexing to recipients. The terms often confused even mothers willing to answer the intrusive questions. One day, I grumbled to Gayle, our unit's sensible lead caseworker, "I hate these sleazy-ass questions we have to ask. I'm always afraid someone is gonna cuss me out for asking them. Besides, these mothers don't know what words like 'putative'(agency-speak for presumed) and 'intercourse' mean and I don't want to be the one to explain them."

Gayle chuckled and said: "Yeah, the only question we don't have to ask was 'Did y'all come?' and 'Was it good for you'? My clients don't know those words, either, so I just started asking them 'Where did y'all do it, how long did y'all do it, how many times, and was he the only one you did it with?'"

Taking my cue from Gayle, that's how I posed the questions after that, but I always felt slimy and squirmy asking them.

After the ADC recipients, the general assistance (GA) clients gave us the most trouble. No one would come out and say it, but they were mainly patients released from mental hospitals. GA was supposed to be temporary, and while getting it, they were supposed to be looking for jobs. Many GA recipients never got better and some tried to fool their caseworkers by endlessly pretending to look for work. Many if not most employers were reluctant to hire the mentally ill so even those who did search for work were usually unsuccessful. Most GA recipients managed to get general assistance forever, or at least until they were re-institutionalized.

We caseworkers dreaded GA visits, as you never knew what you might find or what might find you. One day, Hadley assigned me to visit a recently released recipient in a set of buildings that looked as if they had been built during the Civil War. The building's bricks were black with age and the windows were gray with muck, it had no foundation, and leaned alarmingly. The pitch-black hallway stank with urine and rot. I swallowed my fear, entered and knocked at the door. To my intense terror, the door was flung open by someone who seemed to stand eight feet tall, wearing a torn, dirty, red satin cocktail dress and seven inch red stilettos with the sides busted out. Its head was capped by a humongous bushy fright wig, and the mouth opened revealing jagged, rotting yellow teeth. The nightmare shouted with dead animal breath: "What the hell you want, bitch?"

Despite the dress and heels, I could see the person was or used to be a man. I jumped clean off the floor with fear and turned to run. Just then I heard scratching in the corner near the exit and saw a mangy rat as big as a cat between me and the door. For a split second, I couldn't decide which was scarier-- the wild-eyed drag queen or the nasty-looking rat. One more look over my shoulder at the queen's hostile face and still-cursing mouth made up my mind. I told myself to run past the rat, to not fall or slip or look at it and hit the sidewalk running. Hopefully, nothing would follow me. When I got back to the office, I lied: I wrote in my summary that the recipient wasn't home. I never went back, nor did I call either to discuss a follow-up. The recipient never complained. That case was closed as far as I was concerned.

We all feared the most dangerous clients, those recipients who believed they were entitled to something but then didn't receive it. Caseworkers had been and were attacked verbally and physically if they couldn't make the system work quickly for clients. Every unit was understaffed and had what was called an uncovered load--cases that had no specific caseworker assigned to them. We were all supposed to take a portion of the cases but already overworked, we all dragged our feet. In one of her rare displays of decisiveness, Hadley held a meeting and demanded that each of our four workers take a quarter of the cases because "they" were getting calls from uncovered clients and were unhappy about it.

Among my uncovered cases was a recipient named Roberta Bonds, who had two daughters, both thirteen and both pregnant. I set up a visit. Their home was big, pleasant, sunny and clean. Bonds was a bark-brown, birdlike woman. The two girls, each about six months pregnant, sat silently, gazing morosely at their laps, while Bonds told me their unpleasant and disturbing story. "You know, both these girls is thirteen but they got themselves pregnant. They both stuck hangers up themselves to get rid of their babies even though I didn't know nothing about it. They might have drunk something too, I ain't sure," she said somewhat defensively. "They got little fast girlfriends who told them how to do it but they just ended up making themselves sick as dogs." Bonds knew abortion was illegal. She didn't think there was anything she could do about any damage or even if the babies would be born alive. However, she did believe the daughters should get the new birth payment allowance right then and there.

The Illinois welfare system gave pregnant mothers an additional dollar and change in their monthly budget for extra expenses. The girls had already received that. After birth, the system would subtract the pregnancy allowance, and add about two dollars for additional baby expenses. Bonds wanted the post birth allotments then and there and didn't want to hear a "no."

Shaken by the story but attempting to be firm, I raced through the pat company line that no one could get the birth allotment until birth occurred. Bonds calmly looked me in the eye and said, "Miss Washington, did you hear about the last case worker who had this load before you? He was a nice white guy but he wouldn't give me what I wanted and I had to stab him. He was in the hospital for a long, long time. They put me in Manteno [the local mental hospital] for a few days but they couldn't keep me. I'm not crazy but I can play crazy. You seem like a nice young lady, I'd hate to have to do you the same way."

I looked in her eyes and I could see she wasn't bluffing. She might or might not regret stabbing me, but I would regret it a whole lot. I believed her story about the caseworker. It illustrated that the system wasn't going to punish her if she hurt me. I believed it, because the Charlie rape story had convinced me you could be attacked and no one would care. The system didn't care what happened to Charlie or me. I packed up my tote bag and case materials. Back at the office, I arranged for Bonds to get the two birth allowances. No one caught it then, but a month or so later Hadley confronted me about it. "That family got an extra five dollars or so that they weren't entitled to," she twittered indignantly. 'They' will be really mad about it when they find out. We have rules we have to follow, Kim."

I described the troubling conversation and situation at Bonds' house and admitted I had been both sympathetic to the girl's situation and afraid of Roberta Bonds. I reminded Mrs. Hadley that we weren't even talking about an extra ten dollars, and that it was a one-time only payment. She interrupted me and repeated, "They weren't entitled to that money!"

I blew up. "You didn't even have the decency to tell me she put the last caseworker in the hospital, and that she was crazy, and you're raising hell with me over a few lousy bucks? Get out of my face, Mrs. Hadley!"

She scuttled back to her desk and didn't raise the subject again. I knew she was sneaky and would rat me out to "them", but it was May and I was due to start law school in August so I didn't care.

Two more disquieting incidents had me counting the minutes until I could leave that office. Tank and Broomstick hated Kate, the white caseworker in my unit, because of her outspoken ways. Kate spent most of her time talking about her Communist Party beliefs and railing at how the system screwed the recipients. I had heard Broomstick speak scornfully of Kate's work ("she's lazy!") and her appearance (hippyish) and had seen them both going through her desk when she was in the field. These two black women spoke openly and contemptuously of the recipients and hated anyone, like Kate, who seemed sympathetic to them. Broomstick claimed, "I'm hard on those clients because white folks think we're all like them----lazy and trifling and don't want to work." Both viewed recipients as the scum of the earth, and derided the state system that sustained them. The two saw no contradiction in taking a salary for working with those same people, however.

I believed the two supervisors were hateful in general and had it in for everyone, not just the recipients. Most of the other case workers talked as if they felt the way Tank and Broomstick did. I was sorry for the recipients and understood that many of them were struggling to get their lives in order. In fact, one young client mother of mine was in medical school. I definitely sympathized with the children in the system, regardless of what their parents did or didn't do, should or should not have done.

I had always worried a bit that angry recipients, bent on doing us harm, might come up to the second floor where we all sat even though a posted notice prohibited them from coming upstairs. However, there were no security guards.

One day, a recipient ran upstairs and bounded onto the caseworker floor. She spotted Kate and pummeled her viciously in the head and face with her fists and a large, heavy purse. That day, I returned to the office after being out in the field. The caseworkers were all clustered around, gossiping. Even Mrs. Mink, a splotch of grimy orange, had left her post on the couch and was huddled with the others. Charlie ran over to me, "Washington! You missed it! You know that client who started a bunch of cases with fake names? She came up here and started jacking up Kate because she didn't get one of her checks on time. She beat her with some kind of big ol' heavy satchel she had. They had to take Kate over to Michael Reese [a local hospital]."

When I asked Charlie what Tank and Broom had done to stop the attack, Charlie snorted and shook her head, "You know what those two old bitches are like. They just stood up there and did nothing. It looked to me like Broomstick was even laughing. And Katie was just screaming and falling down. It's a damn shame, Washington, what this office is like. They don't give a shit about nobody."

Apparently no one called the police. The attacker finally ran downstairs and out of the building. One of the younger workers took Kate to the emergency room. I asked myself: *Why hadn't the supervisors stopped the attack? And why were they smiling or laughing during the attack? Why did no one call the police or report it after the fact? Why was there no security in the first place? Did they hate Kate that much? What if the recipient had been carrying a gun or a knife and had attacked others?*

The managers never mentioned the attack on Kate nor made any attempt to warn caseworkers. They didn't institute any new safety or security precautions. Kate returned to work about a week later, face swollen and bruised purple. The attack had left her nose broken, her jaw unaligned and her eye injured. When I expressed my regret and anger about the incident, she said, speaking slowly and without fire

The Chit'lin Coast

for once, "Oh, well. The client was just angry because her check was late. And the supervisors don't like me very much, I guess. But I've got good news. I'm getting married!" I had never heard Kate mention a boyfriend and even wondered whether she might be gay. When I asked who she was marrying, she told me it was someone the leaders of her local Communist Party unit had instructed her to marry. She didn't mention his name.

She went on to explain that the Party bosses thought her marriage would be good for the cause and enhance their ability to meet Party goals. She admitted to having only met her groom-to-be once before. She wasn't worried though: "We have to fight the war and racism and sexism and I think we can do that together even if we don't know one another." I started to ask her how she could marry a stranger, and what about love. But seeing her battered but determined face, I decided it was a topic best left unexplored.

About a month before I was due to leave, a frail, pale, white caseworker named Nancy stood up suddenly in the middle of the day and started running around the periphery of the room, moaning and wailing. Nancy always wore a long, granny dress which slowed but did not stop her. No one moved or went to her. Everyone kept working and few even glanced toward her. For several hours, Nancy orbited the room groaning, grunting and mumbling unintelligibly. Watching Nancy stumble by, Gayle said, "This happened last year, too. All of a sudden she just goes off. No one knows what causes it. Someone told me she's been in at least one mental institution, but, you know, she seemed like she got over it pretty fast and was okay." Apparently, because of the supposed quick recovery, no one felt it was necessary to delve beneath the surface and see if she truly was recovered or even call her family.

I didn't know Nancy well, but I started to go over to her. Gayle placed her hand on my arm and shook her head. Nancy ran around until someone in her unit led her out to an ambulance. She was lifted inside and they sped away. She never returned while I worked there nor was she mentioned.

After this incident, I felt like fleeing immediately and not waiting until August. I had been there not even a year but it seemed unending, oppressive. I had earned as much as I was going to earn and had saved most of it. It would have to be enough to pay my expenses for the school year. Although I was only twenty, I had worked for two large institutions before—the University of Illinois and the Post Office. They were, for the most part, huge, soulless, detached, and antagonistic to the interests of their workers and clients. Still, this job was worse. No one's efforts seemed to make any difference in the lives of the clients. The job sandwiched the workers between the indifferent system and the angry recipients. The job made everyone nuts.

I felt guilty--I hadn't made any real efforts to help anyone, other than mechanically doing the work. Even though I hadn't been personally harmed and liked many of my co-workers and many of the recipients, I knew I wouldn't miss them or be missed. I came home from this pressure cooker with a banging headache every day that couldn't be erased with booze or talks with my mother who was resigned to the chaos of the job. I lay in bed, sleepless many nights, while thoughts of Mrs. Hadley, the recipients, their devastated neighborhoods and miserable lives, Tank and Broom, the other caseworkers, and "the list" circled my brain in a dead heat with Nancy, the "crazy" caseworker. Looking back, I don't think my experience at the state welfare agency changed me intrinsically. It made me a bit more knowledgeable about and sensitive to the issue of welfare and the people in the system. The welfare system will always be discussed, argued about and condemned, usually by people who have never had to depend on it. At the time though, I told myself that because of this experience, I would know more about real-world jobs and the types of people who work them than did the average law school student. That turned out to be true.

Just before I left, I talked to a male caseworker who had been in law school at the University of Chicago but had dropped out. When I asked him why, he said, "Kim, reading those class materials every night was like reading your insurance policy over and over again. I just couldn't stand it." For some reason, his description of law school was immensely soothing. I didn't care how hard and boring law school was going to be, I couldn't wait to get there. I was tired of the constant tension and incipient jeopardy of the caseworking world. The world of dry lectures and even drier books could not come fast enough for me.

My hope was for the peace of academia, coupled with my long held desire to escape my family and Chicago. I would find a doctor somewhere that would remove the dreaded, almost two year old breast lump. I was eager to leave and leave forever.

L.A. Whitaker
September 2014

Made in the USA
Lexington, KY
21 May 2015